American Diaries

ZELLIE BLAKE

LOWELL, MASSACHUSETTS, 1834

by Kathleen Duey

Aladdin Paperbacks

New York   London   Toronto   Sydney   Singapore

For Richard
For Ever

First Aladdin Paperbacks edition May 2002

Copyright © 2002 by Kathleen Duey

ALADDIN PAPERBACKS
An imprint of Simon & Schuster
Children's Publishing Division
1230 Avenue of the Americas
New York, NY 10020

The text for this book was set in Fairfield.
Printed and bound in the United States of America
10 9 8 7 6 5 4 3 2

Library of Congress Control Number: 2002100840
ISBN 0-689-84405-0

American Diaries

ZELLIE BLAKE

LOWELL, MASSACHUSETTS, 1834

Thursday, February 20, 1834
Lowell, Massachusetts

My fourth day here and finally a moment to write . . .

I have finished fetching six buckets of water, which is what it takes to fill the big kitchen barrel. Everything about housework is harder here than it was at home. It is a very big house! But I am lucky to have gotten the position, I know.

I should have asked Reverend Albee and the neighbors at home for letters of recommendation, but I never even thought of it. People are scared off when I tell the truth about having no family left. I tried fourteen other places before this one and was turned away from all of them—many people were just plain rude.

Mrs. Gird is still asking me to spy on the girls for her. I don't want to do it. These mill girls all seem nice enough. Most talk and laugh, some of them borrow each other's clothes. They all help each other dress their hair or find a missing hairpin. It's like a huge family of sisters, I guess.

Some are quiet, some noisy, but all do their parts; all are polite and busy with their needlework or their books in the evenings. Most days they work twelve or thirteen hours. Saturdays, Mrs. Gird said, they work a little less. And the work is easy, really.

I heard two girls talking about being homesick when I was carrying their breakfast plates to them. I am homesick too.

Little good it will do me. With Grandmamma dead and gone, I have no home anymore.

The girls had their heads together over breakfast this morning, whispering. After they had all left for the mill, Mrs. Gird asked me to find out what they were talking about.

I don't think I can refuse to try.

Here's what I know:

1. The girls are whispering about something.
2. Mrs. Gird told me I am to keep my ears open and to find out what.
3. If I can do that, she says, she might decide I am worth keeping.
4. If I spy on the girls, they will likely notice. Then they will surely hate me.
5. But if I don't tattle on them, Mrs. Gird might very well let me go. I have no choice. These girls care nothing for me, so why should I care for them?
6. Last but most, as Grandmamma would say when she made her lists, I cannot lose my employment with Mrs. Gird—at least not until spring. I felt as if I would die of cold walking the fifteen miles from home to Lowell.

If Mrs. Gird let me go, what would I do? Try to get back to Billerica?

I'd have nowhere to stay and Grandmamma's grave is the only thing I would care about there. The farm is gone, gone, gone. Mr. Spears sold it off to that German family so fast, I know he must have been talking to them about it while Grandmamma was sick. He could have waited just a little, could have let me clear out in my own time.

I have so far managed to preserve my remaining ninety-seven cents. I worked bits and pieces for farm-wives who fed me on my way, walking to Lowell. If this boardinghouse employment lasts, I will spend a little money soon. I will have to.

My shoes are worn through, my coat is falling to tatters. Someone is going to think I am a runaway if I can't get a little fixed up—that worries me if I leave Massachusetts for Philadelphia. What if I got hauled south and couldn't prove I was born free?

I do wish I could work in the mills, but there's not a single other Negro girl that I can see doing anything but domestic work here in Lowell.

And even if they hired Negro girls, most of the mill girls are several years older than I am—fifteen or sixteen, some in their twenties. But there are jobs for younger ones; there must be. I have seen them in the mornings, filing through the Merrimack factory gates with the rest of the older girls.

The girls all went to church on the Sabbath. I didn't. There is a colored church-meeting held in town and I will go next Sunday. I was so tired from scrubbing floors I just slept until seven and decided to skip it. Grandmamma wouldn't approve, I know. She never let me miss church or school. And she would be sick about me scrubbing and changing linens all day. She wanted me to be a teacher, but that can't happen now. . . .

I'll never be able to go to school again.

Oh, dear, I hear Mrs. Gird coming down the stairs . . . heavy-footed as an ox. Better hide my book.

CHAPTER ONE

Zellie slid her journal-book back into her satchel and clasped the little brass lock between the handles shut. The key was on a slender silver chain Grandmamma had given her and she slipped it back around her neck.

The slow, heavy footsteps got closer. Zellie jumped up to set the satchel by the wall, then stacked the neatly folded blankets Mrs. Gird had provided for her on top of it. Zellie hoped that Mrs. Gird would give her a ticked mattress to use before long. The floor before the hearth was *hard*.

Zellie whirled around and shoved the last bit of her breakfast bread into her mouth and washed it down with a swallow of milk.

Mrs. Gird appeared in the kitchen doorway an instant later, her stern, sour face shiny with perspiration. "Finished?"

"Yes'm," answered Zellie.

"Good." Mrs. Gird was glancing around the kitchen.

The first day there, Zellie had tried to be polite and friendly. She had watched Mrs. Gird straining curd into her cheese molds and had started to tell her about how Grandmamma had made cheese without salt or sheep's gut.

Mrs. Gird had stared at her as though one of the kitchen brooms had suddenly begun to speak. So Zellie had given it up.

Mrs. Gird was standing now with her hands on her hips, scowling as her eyes flickered over the kitchen. The scowl seemed to be her usual expression, so it was hard to tell if she was upset over something or not.

Zellie looked around. She had blown out all but three of the astral lamps. The sun was almost up. She had swept the hearth free of crumbs and splatters. She'd raked up a bucket of ashes and had dumped them onto the snowy road behind the boardinghouse. She had scrubbed the floor before the hearth and had scraped the roast-of-beef leftovers from last night's supper into the beginnings of a soup for noon dinner.

The drainboard was clean. Zellie had washed the dishes the night before, of course. The china was thinner than any she had ever handled and it made her nervous, at first, but she was becoming less afraid.

Fifty girls at every meal and she hadn't broken anything. She hadn't even chipped one plate or cup.

"Linens are to be changed today," Mrs. Gird said abruptly. "Four days early, but I want to start doing them Thursdays, not Mondays like all the rest. The laundress says she'll go cheaper if I fill an empty day for her."

Zellie blinked. The idea of changing laundry day from Monday to Thursday would never have occurred to her. Mrs. Gird was more clever than she had thought.

Mrs. Gird cleared her throat. "Start on the third floor."

Zellie nodded, but her stomach tightened.

"On with you, then," Mrs. Gird said, making a shooing motion like someone would at a dog.

Zellie bit her lip and hurried to wash her plate and cup.

"I meant to tell you," Mrs. Gird said from behind her. "Don't set those on the drainboard today."

Zellie stared at her.

"From now on, I want you to put them in that old cracker box, down below."

Trying not to look upset or even surprised, Zellie set her dishes into the box on the floor.

"I don't believe in slavery," Mrs. Gird said as Zellie was straightening up. Zellie turned, wary.

"My people are from the South, but I don't think

slavery is right," Mrs. Gird went on. "I believe that Jesus must hate the slavers."

Zellie gave her a tiny nod. Abolition was not something she wanted to discuss with a white woman or, at least, not with *this* white woman. Grandmamma had taught her to be careful with strangers of all sorts. Some were grand. Others were dangerous. Most fell in between.

Mrs. Gird sighed heavily. "But I *do* believe in separation."

Zellie tipped her head slightly, a tiny motion that only said she had heard, not what she thought about any of this.

"So I don't want you mixing up your dishes with the rest and I don't want you getting too friendly with the girls," Mrs. Gird said evenly. She wiped the back of her hand across her forehead. It was chilly in the house, but she was perspiring. "You must certainly be polite. But no more than that. Understood?"

Zellie nodded again. What else could she do?

"Are you sure you haven't overheard anything?" Mrs. Gird asked.

Zellie shook her head, wishing desperately that she had something to tell her.

Mrs. Gird sighed and her frown deepened. This was clearly not what she had hoped to hear. "I hired you without letters of introduction or recommendation," she said heavily. "I hope I won't regret that."

"They have been whispering, some of them," Zellie said, telling the truth. "But when I come close, they stop."

Mrs. Gird nodded. "They will, for a while. Then they will forget you are there. They're like a flock of sparrows." She laughed aloud.

Zellie didn't answer. Mrs. Gird was probably right. The girls would get used to seeing her about. And if she was silent and never got friendly, they would start to forget she was there—like a chair or a hat rack. The folks Grandmamma had worked for had argued in front of her, had discussed family troubles in the parlor while she stood five feet away in the kitchen. Of course Grandmamma had never repeated anything she'd heard.

"Just mind that you stay quiet and don't talk to the young ladies much and we will get on fine," Mrs. Gird said.

"Yes, Ma'am," Zellie said because she knew she was expected to.

"Now get those linens changed!" Mrs. Gird clapped her hands. Zellie jumped, jolted out of her thoughts. Mrs. Gird smiled. "So, you can look lively when you want to."

Angry, Zellie lifted her chin. "Where will I find the clean linens, Ma'am?"

Mrs. Gird pointed. "There are linen chests in the storeroom. And bring the soiled ones back down. They need to be set out for the laundress's wagon. Her son drives it around."

Zellie nodded, then hesitated.

Mrs. Gird frowned. "What are you waiting for?"

"Only to make sure you were done instructing me," Zellie said politely. She kept her eyes on the floor most of the time. Mrs. Gird might think Jesus hated slavery, but that didn't mean she shared His opinion, not down deep in her soul.

"I am finished," Mrs. Gird said heavily. "I'll be in my room if you need to ask anything."

Zellie hurried out of the kitchen and started up the long hall. She could hear Mrs. Gird's footsteps on the wooden floor behind her as she passed the closed door of the little parlor. No one had used it for a few days—none of the girls had had a gentleman caller.

Zellie nearly ran toward the storeroom, eager to put distance between herself and Mrs. Gird. She opened the heavy door and stepped inside. Then for the hundredth time, Zellie wished that her Auntie Persis had not gone to Philadelphia. It had been two years and she hadn't written, not once. Grandmamma had been so hurt. But she had said that Auntie Persis never pined for anything that wasn't right beside her.

Zellie knew that really meant that Auntie Persis had never given two shakes about anyone except herself. It made no sense. Grandmamma was generous and loving, so how could one of her daughters grow up so selfish? Zellie shook her head. "And now Auntie Persis doesn't even know that Grandmamma is dead," she whispered to herself.

"Do you need help in there?"

Mrs. Gird's voice came up the hall and made Zellie whirl around to face the door. Her toe caught the edge of a stack of boxes and they swayed. She managed to catch the top box before they all fell over.

"No, Ma'am," she called back.

There was only silence, then the sound of Mrs. Gird's footsteps. Zellie exhaled, setting the box back. The lid had come off. It was full of bits of old sisal rope. Grandmamma had loved to get hold of old rope for scouring pots and scrubbing floors.

Zellie settled the box and pushed thoughts of her grandmother aside so she wouldn't start crying. Then she ran to the linen trunks and piled a stack of folded bedclothes as high as she could carry. When she came out of the storeroom, Mrs. Gird was nowhere to be seen.

Zellie started up the first flight of stairs and immediately wished she hadn't brought such a big load of linens. She couldn't see the stairs without turning sideways.

Feeling silly for walking like a crab, Zellie made her way slowly upward. On the first two landings, she stopped for a second and hitched the stack of linens higher in her arms. The last thing she wanted to do was to drop any of them. Mrs. Gird would have a tizzy.

On the third floor, Zellie ignored the window on the landing and went to the first of the three rooms. For a long second, she stood outside the closed door. She had never been in someone else's bedroom that she could recall, except the one Grandmamma and Auntie Persis had shared. But she had never had to hire out before, either. Grandmamma had done that. Zellie had tended their garden and the chickens and their cow. She had done everything on their little farm. Except the farm hadn't really been theirs, of course.

Zellie shook her head to clear her thoughts. It just seemed so odd to be changing a stranger's bed. "Get used to it," she whispered to herself.

Shifting the linens to free one hand, she turned the latch and eased the door open. Then she hesitated again. The room was heavy with the scent of lavender sachets. There were three beds, which meant that six girls stayed in this room.

Zellie made her way through the room, stepping around a hair trunk. The black-and-white cowhide that covered it was worn in places. She lifted the linens high to clear the stacks of trunks and cases. She set the linens on the first bed she could reach, then turned again, rubbing her sweaty hands down her apron.

There was a window on the other side of the

room. Zellie stared at it, listening to her heart pounding. Then she forced herself to walk closer to it. After a moment, she made herself look downward. The flowerbeds along the side of the house were laden with mounds of snow. She raised her eyes. She could see the Pawtucket Canal. The water was dark and sluggish, but not frozen over.

She pulled in a long breath, fighting the dizzy-sick feeling she always got when she was up high. She turned away after a few seconds.

This was something else she was going to have to get used to as quickly as she could. A lot of the buildings in Lowell were several stories high.

I'll look out again in a minute, she told herself as she fled back across the room, but she knew she wouldn't.

Being up high had always made her stomach sick. She had never climbed trees with the Wilson boys when she was little. She had told them it wasn't proper for a young lady. It wasn't, but that wasn't why she refused.

Zellie hauled in a deep breath. She focused her thoughts, facing the comfort of the solid wall. Grandmamma had taught her that every job contained tricks and puzzles. If you could figure them out, you could do the work in half the time.

The biggest puzzle in this room was the lack of space—even to walk. The beds were close together, and the girls' belongings made it almost impossible to move around.

It made sense to strip the linens first, Zellie thought, and get all the soiled laundry out in the hall. Then she would make up the beds with the fresh sheets, one by one.

Maneuvering around the trunks, she pulled the bedclothes free of the first two beds and piled them out in the hall. Then she went back and started on the third bed.

The bolster and the blankets came away easily. But the linen sheet stuck on something and Zellie tugged harder. It still wouldn't come free.

Crawling onto the bed, Zellie peered down behind the mattress. The straw stuffing crackled beneath her weight as she bent down. Zellie saw the problem. There was a writing box tucked between the bed and the wall.

Zellie sat back on her heels. She didn't really want to touch the box. But there was no way to change the linens without pulling it up and out of the way.

Zellie glanced at the door. The girls would not be home until dinnertime. The factory bell rang at noon—hours away. She reached down to get the box and freed it gently, careful not to scratch it or the wall.

She rocked back on her heels, intending to set

the box carefully on one of the chests of drawers while she made the bed. But she lost her balance and tangled one foot in the folds of the linen. Instead of standing up, she fell sideways. As she reached out to break her fall, the box came out of her hands and sailed across the room.

CHAPTER TWO

Zellie wriggled out of the twisted sheet, hopping backward on one foot. She could see the box. It had spilled but wasn't broken. A relieved giggle rose in her throat. Then she pressed her fingers against her mouth and tiptoed to the doorway.

She listened, barely breathing. There was no sound from below, no voice, no thudding footsteps. Nothing. Knowing she had been lucky—not clever— Zellie turned back into the room.

The box had landed, flipped open, then rolled, stopping against the foot of a round-topped travel trunk. The letters and blank paper it contained ran in a tumbled row along the floor.

Zellie picked them up, starting at one end, glad they were still in order. If the girl who owned the box noticed that her letters had been discombobulated . . .

Zellie hesitated, staring at the sheets of paper in her hand. A few were blank, but the ones that had writing on them did not look like letters. Zellie looked closer. They were lists of names—girls' names.

Puzzled, Zellie leafed through the sheets. In addition to the eight or ten filled with girls' names, there was a cover sheet with a short inscription. It was upside down, the writing fanciful and scrolled. Maybe the girl was getting married soon and thinking about guests. Zellie smiled. Whoever she was, she had a lot of friends!

The sound of heavy footsteps below made Zellie flinch. She stacked the papers as carefully as she could, turning the top sheet around to match the rest as she set them inside the box. As she was closing the lid, the top sheet's lines of script leapt out at her.

These are the ones in this house who say they will come with us. Tell no one.

Most loyally yours,
Lydia

"Getting started up there?" Mrs. Gird's voice came booming up the stairs.

Zellie shoved the box beneath the bed and ripped off the linens. She pitched them into the hall. As Mrs. Gird huffed her way up the last few steps, Zellie was tucking in the top sheet on the bed farthest from the window.

"Clever girl," Mrs. Gird said as she looked in the doorway. She had a bundle of linens in her arms and stood sideways to see over them. "Stripping them all at once saves time."

Zellie nodded, her face polite and calm. She was not about to let Mrs. Gird know that she had been doing anything except her proper work. And she hadn't *meant* to be, anyway.

"I'll carry the dirty ones down and leave these across the hall," Mrs. Gird said.

Zellie nodded. "Yes, Ma'am."

"It takes me an hour per floor," she said as she started down the stairs. The planked floor creaked and groaned beneath her feet. "You should be much faster."

Determined to show Mrs. Gird that she was worthy of hiring permanently, Zellie flung herself into her work. She changed the three beds, put the writing box back where she found it, then hurried across the hall.

The second room was even more crowded than the first. One of the girls had a small library of books. Zellie wanted to look at them, but knew she shouldn't.

As she worked, Zellie passed from one room to another, thinking about the odd inscription she'd read. "Tell no one," she whispered aloud. It sounded like something someone in a novel would say. Maybe it was some sort of club they were forming and they were being secretive, just for fun.

She would not risk repeating it to Mrs. Gird until she was sure it meant something—and she had overheard it elsewhere, too. Admitting that she had touched one of the girls' things—even by accident—would be foolish. The next time something was missing, she'd be accused of stealing.

Zellie finished the third floor as quickly as she could. Then she went down the stairs, just managing to carry the loose heap of dirty linens. She glanced out the landing window, but then quickly looked away.

Mrs. Gird was in the kitchen again. Zellie could hear the steady huffing of the hearth bellows, and the smell of bubbling stew was already drifting down the hallway.

On her way back up the stairs, Zellie tried to imagine Mrs. Gird humming and smiling as she cooked. Grandmamma always had.

As she worked, Zellie played at guessing which of the girls she had noticed at meals in the dining hall lived in which of the rooms. One room had a dresser top positively rainbowed in hair ribbons. Many of the girls had two or three, but this girl must have spent a substantial portion of her wages on ribbons. And she had laid them out in a careful, unwrinkled row for all the others to admire . . . or envy.

Zellie touched a green ribbon with the tip of a single finger. It was silk, she was sure. Made somewhere else in the world, shipped to Boston, then brought here by railroad or canal boat or maybe carried in a peddler's wagon.

For an instant, Zellie imagined the long road the

ribbon had traveled, just to end up on a mill girl's chest of drawers. She shook her head. It was amazing to think about. She smiled, then went back to work.

In the next room, there was a makeshift library. This girl had made a little shelf of an apple crate. There were seven books upon it!

Zellie ached to pull out the books to see if she could read them—or if they were too hard. But she wouldn't, not without asking. She would never have touched the writing box if she hadn't had to.

"And if Mrs. Gird found out you were asking to look at books, being friendly, you'd be out the back door," she scolded herself aloud. Then she shook her head.

Grandmamma had talked to herself a lot. Old people were *supposed* to. "Not twelve-year-old girls," Zellie whispered, then grinned. Talking to herself was a habit she'd gotten from Grandmamma and it made her feel less lonely. So as long as no one overheard her, she didn't care if it was odd.

In the last room, one of the girls had left her trunk standing open. Zellie could see three dresses, neatly folded, and two spare bonnets. She wondered which one of the girls owned them. It had to be some-one who wasn't sending money home to support a family. Maybe an orphaned girl?

Zellie's eyes stung. She had no family herself now—no one to send money to. No one to go home to. No one at all, unless she could somehow find

Auntie Persis. The stinging turned to tears and Zellie swiped at her eyes.

"Are you finished?" Mrs. Gird shouted from below.

"Almost, Ma'am," Zellie shouted back. She was grateful for the interruption this time. Whenever she started thinking about being alone, her heart felt cold and small, like when she stood on the edge of a high place and looked down. She felt helpless and scared and she hated feeling that way.

"I need you to run an errand for me!" Mrs. Gird shouted as Zellie gathered up the last pile of soiled linen and started down the stairs.

"Coming!" Zellie shouted back.

Breathless, she added the linens to the pile in the storeroom, made sure she had closed the chests that held the clean ones, and whirled to run down the hall toward the kitchen.

Mrs. Gird was leaning over the huge cast-iron cauldron. The pot was so big and so heavy that Zellie was sure Mrs. Gird had never taken it down to wash it. How could she?

"I want you to run into town," Mrs. Gird was saying. "And I do mean *run*."

"Yes, Ma'am," Zellie said politely.

Mrs. Gird didn't exactly smile at her, but her scowl seemed to ease a little.

"I'm fast," Zellie added. She was already pulling

off her apron and wishing the soles of her shoes weren't full of holes.

"Take this." Mrs. Gird was holding out something.

Zellie stretched out her hand, expecting to be given a few coins to buy whatever it was that Mrs. Gird needed. But it wasn't coins. They were tiny gold buttons.

"Go to the corner of Central and Hurd Streets. It's just down past the General Stage Office," Mrs. Gird said. "The American Coffeehouse is in that same building—if you get lost ask for either one—everyone in town knows where they are." She handed Zellie the buttons. "The shop is a millinery. There's a hat painted on the sign. Tell Gillian O'Brien I want all ten of these sewn in around the crown of the hat she's making for me—they'll set off the ribbon."

Zellie took the buttons carefully.

Mrs. Gird pointed at the rag bin beneath the drainboard. "Tie them up in a bit of cloth so you don't lose them. My sister's getting married," she added, and almost smiled. "I'm getting a new hat for church."

Zellie started to smile back, but when she reached into the rag bin and looked down, she noticed her dishes in the box on the floor. Her smile stiffened.

"Hurry right back," Mrs. Gird added. "We still have a lot to do before the girls come waltzing home for noon dinner."

"Yes, Ma'am," Zellie answered. She got her coat.

"That won't keep you warm," Mrs. Gird said. "You'd better run." She winked.

Zellie nodded without answering. Being cold wasn't funny.

"Hurry," Mrs. Gird chided as Zellie went out the back door.

Zellie paused on the little porch to button up her coat and slip the rag that held the buttons into her bodice. Then she stepped down into the snow.

There was a worn path to the street and she was grateful. The snow would seep through the holes in the soles of her shoes, but at least it wouldn't come in through the tops, too.

A farm wagon was passing and she looked up at the driver. He didn't look away. "Sir?" Zellie called. "Could you direct me to Central and Hurd?"

The man pointed. "Cut through there, past the print works. Turn down Warthen and follow it to Merrimack. Turn left there, then right on Central, then straight on till you see Hurd."

Zellie smiled her thanks and set off, walking fast, repeating the directions to herself.

"New shoes," she said to herself as she followed the path that led past the smelly print works. "I need new shoes." But she knew that shoes would cost at least a dollar. It was going to take some time to save up that much money.

Zellie looked at the red brick building. It smelled

awful from the dyes they used to print the colors on the cloth.

Grandmamma had been proud of the Lowell calico she'd bought a few summers past. It had worn well. "You would have loved Lowell," Zellie whispered, talking to her grandmother. "You would love how neat and perfect it all is."

Grandmamma would have been asking someone in the print works to let her watch, too, Zellie knew. She would have wanted to know how it was done. Zellie looked at the snow, thinking about her grandmother, aching to have her back.

CHAPTER THREE

Zellie came out of the maze of buildings and stood still. There was no street sign. Was this Warthen? In a week or two, she would know her way around. But now, she was completely confused.

A man was walking toward her, his cap pulled down over his ears. His hands were buried in his coat front.

"Sir?" Zellie asked.

He slowed and looked at her. "Yes?"

"Can you tell me how to get to the American Coffeehouse? I don't know this town at all."

"See that?" He pointed, jabbing a finger into the cold winter air, then met her eyes. Zellie followed his gesture and saw a church with a tall, squared spire on one end. "That's St. Anne's Episcopal," said the man. "Go past it until you see Central and turn down toward the canal." He nodded briskly and set off before she could thank him.

Zellie watched him go, then went on, walking fast.

Central was wide, rutted with wagon tracks. There were buildings along both sides of the street. She heard a cow lowing somewhere in the distance and felt her stomach tighten. If Grandmamma were alive, if they had been at home, it'd be about time to milk Polly.

Zellie kept walking. The dark water in the Pawtucket Canal rushed along the narrow banks, heading toward the mills that crouched at the edge of the Concord River. Not far below them, the water flowed into the Merrimack. Zellie could hear the distant splashing of the water as the waterwheels churned in their endless circles.

Zellie held still a moment. She liked the sound of the river. She liked a lot of things about Lowell. The red brick of the buildings stood out against the white snowy fields beyond the Merrimack. The bare, gray tree limbs were piled high with snow.

She started walking again, adding to the list. She liked the stagecoaches that went through town every afternoon. She had seen them only from a distance but even from afar, they were beautiful, the horses blowing clouds of steam from their muzzles.

"It'd be grand to ride in a coach some day," Zellie whispered to herself. Maybe she could save her money for a fare to Philadelphia. She could find Auntie Persis and . . .

"And what?" she asked aloud. Auntie Persis had

left to get *away* from her and Grandmamma. She had wanted to be on her own.

As Zellie passed the stage office, she looked up and down the road, hoping to see one of the six-horsed coaches coming up the street.

She didn't.

There were only plain, common farm wagons. The first was loaded with sacks of flour. The horses were lop-eared and clopped along half asleep. The second was filled with crates of chickens. The clucking faded as she turned down Hurd Street.

The millinery was a little shop. Inside it smelled dusty and faintly like chalk and damp wool. It was gloriously warm. A little stove burned in one corner.

Zellie loosened her coat to let the warmth in faster. There was a tiny silver bell on the counter next to the cash box. She picked it up and rang it lightly.

"I'll be right there," a woman called from behind a half-closed door. Zellie recognized the melody of an Irish accent.

Fiddling with the bundle of buttons in her bodice, Zellie waited. The little shop was crowded with rolls of cloth and millinery dress forms and baskets of thread and lace trims.

Mrs. O'Brien sewed as well as making hats, Zellie saw. Women who came here had a choice of silk or wool or cotton cloth in three or four different colors each.

On a form in the corner, Zellie saw a white dress

taking shape. The rows of tiny tucks in the bodice were straight, perfectly sewn, each stitch so tiny it was nearly invisible.

Zellie reached out to touch the cloth, the magically precise stitching.

"Oh! Are your hands clean?"

The voice startled Zellie into turning around. "Yes, Ma'am," she said quickly, trying keep her eyes down. It was hard. The woman was the whitest, palest person she had ever seen. It was as though her skin had frosted over in a storm and never thawed out. Blue veins in her temples stood out.

"I apologize for touching it," Zellie said, her heart speeding up. If this woman told Mrs. Gird she'd just walked in and had her hands all over someone else's dress and—

"And I apologize. I truly didn't mean to give you such a start," said the woman.

Zellie looked up. Maybe she could just do her errand and leave and the woman wouldn't think to tell Mrs. Gird. "Pardon me, Mrs. O'Brien," she said politely. "You are Mrs. O'Brien, aren't you?"

The woman nodded slowly and gestured toward the white dress. "It's a wedding dress and it has taken me hours to make, what with my poor eyes as bad as they are now. But you jumped, poor dear. So long as your hands are clean, there's no harm done at all."

Zellie hesitated, unsure what to say. Mrs. O'Brien

seemed very polite, but polite didn't always mean kind. And she might tell Mrs. Gird about this, if Zellie was even a little disrespectful. Zellie introduced herself, then lowered her eyes. "You have no cause to apologize, Ma'am" she said carefully. "I had no right to touch the dress. I was admiring the stitching."

Mrs. O'Brien smiled. "What fine manners! Tell your mother for me that she is doing a lovely job of raising you."

Zellie tried to smile, but she couldn't. Her eyes started to sting. She blinked, and turned her head to the side, fighting tears.

"Are you all right?" Mrs. O'Brien asked, her face wrinkling with concern. Her skin crinkled like twisted parchment. For the first time Zellie realized that she was at least thirty-five or forty years old, maybe more. She was *old*.

"Have I said something?" Mrs. O'Brien asked.

Zellie shook her head. "My Grandmamma died about two weeks ago. She was all the family I had left. But she taught me manners, yes, Ma'am."

The woman made a soft sound and came out from behind the counter. Without so much as a pardon me or any other kind of warning, she put her arms around Zellie and held her close. "I am so sorry, dear," she said quietly. "My folks died early on, too. You will find your own way. I did."

Zellie held very still. No one had hugged her

since Grandmamma. She had *never* been held like this by a frosty skinned white woman. It was strange. She had no idea what to say. She expected Mrs. O'Brien to turn loose of her in a second or two—but the old woman did the exact opposite. She began to rock back and forth, humming a little.

Zellie's eyes welled up and over and before she could stop herself, she was crying.

"It will be all right," Mrs. O'Brien said. "It will." She tugged one of Zellie's braids gently and then stroked her hair.

Zellie fought not to cry harder. She sniffled, embarrassed. What in the world was she doing, crying like this with a complete stranger of a white woman? She leaned back and looked up at Mrs. O'Brien.

The old woman's eyes were heavy with tears. "Well, now I owe you another apology," she said, wiping at her eyes. "I have a terrible headache today, so bad I cannot work. And tears are contagious, you know. I've been feeling sorry for myself, anyway, all day."

Zellie stood still as Mrs. O'Brien released her and stepped back, patting her silvery hair. She smiled awkwardly. Zellie fumbled at her bodice again and finally managed to pull out the knotted rag.

"Mrs. Gird sent me with these buttons," she said, lifting her chin.

Mrs. O'Brien had a handkerchief and was dabbing at her eyes. She offered it to Zellie.

Zellie put out her hand and they made an exchange—the handkerchief for the bundle of buttons. She wiped her eyes quickly. The handkerchief had a lace edge and it smelled of some flowery pomade.

"She said to tell you that she wants all of them sewn around the crown," Zellie told her.

"How is she today?" Mrs. O'Brien asked. "Pleasant and joyful?"

Zellie had no idea what to say.

"Grumpy as usual?" Mrs. O'Brien whispered, arching her brows.

Zellie smiled a little, but didn't dare nod. It was not her place to call Mrs. Gird grumpy—at least not out loud.

"Bertha Gird has not been content with anything as long as I have known her," said Mrs. O'Brien.

Zellie could see a joking twinkle in Mrs. O'Brien's eyes and she wanted to smile. But she was afraid to.

"I am working for her now," she said carefully. "I hope. She says she just needs me for a few days, but I am working hard and hoping."

Mrs. O'Brien nodded. "And your manners and your discretion are perfect. But you know what I mean. Not even hearing that our own dear Senator Daniel Webster will visit Lowell cheered her up. . . . And she worships that old Whig."

Zellie's eyes widened. "He's coming here? When?"

Mrs. O'Brien shrugged. "Soon, they say. We get them all, you know. David Crocket is going to tour the town this summer, I was told. Henry Clay was here last October."

Zellie blinked.

"Have you been here long?" Mrs. O'Brien asked.

Zellie shook her head. She didn't want to tell the whole dreary tale. So she just lifted her chin. "I was in Billerica most my life. People said there was work here."

Mrs. O'Brien nodded. "Great things are happening here, Zellie," Mrs. O'Brien said. "All these girls working to support themselves and their families, standing tall and independent and strong. It's inspiring."

"I want to work in the mills," Zellie said without thinking.

Mrs. O'Brien nodded. "If ever people of all colors do work side-by-side every day, it'll be in Massachusetts." Her face brightened. "No one hates slavery more than we do. Have you met any of the Lewis family yet?"

Zellie shook her head. "I haven't met anyone."

"They are lovely Negro people, moved up from Boston. They've been famous speech-making anti-slavery workers for years. They came here and started in on improving the schools." She shook her head. "I admire them. They are a family of courage and spirit."

Mrs. O'Brien stopped talking and pressed one hand to her forehead. She closed her eyes and sighed.

"Grandmamma said cold was best for head-aches," Zellie said. "I could go out and get you a cup full of snow. You just wrap it up in soft cloth . . ." She looked around the shop. Near the workbench the floor was littered with scraps.

Mrs. O'Brien smiled wanly. "I'll try anything."

Zellie went out, grateful for the rush of cold air. It startled her into thinking hard. "I shouldn't be chat-ting," she said quietly to herself. "I have to get back before Mrs. Gird gets impatient."

But as she waded through the muddy snow on Central and crossed to the far side to find a handful that was clean, she admitted to herself that she didn't want to go back to the boardinghouse.

Mrs. O'Brien was *nice*. She reminded Zellie of Grandmamma. She was just plain kind.

"Oh, my," Mrs. O'Brien said as Zellie came back in. "If this works I shall be so grateful."

Zellie found a scrap of cloth big enough and rolled the snow up in it, folding the ends in and tying them with a piece of thread. "Here," she said.

Mrs. O'Brien smiled and pressed the cloth to her eyes. "It gets bad when I try to work for too long. My sight is not what it used to be."

Zellie glanced at the stitching on the dress she had touched. "Those stitches are tiny. I could never do that."

Mrs. O'Brien laughed. "Yes, you could. You come over in the evenings after Mrs. Gird is finished with you and I will teach you to sew. Every woman should be able to sew well."

Zellie caught her breath. "Would you really teach me?"

Mrs. O'Brien lowered the cloth and nodded. "I would. I teach simple millinery classes to the mill girls to earn a few extra pennies. There's one tonight. You won't need to pay. We'll call it a trade for this." She smiled and opened her eyes. "Oh, Zellie, it's helping a little."

Zellie smiled.

Mrs. O'Brien pressed the little bag of snow against her eyes again. It was melting, the cloth was soaking through.

"I better go back now," Zellie said.

Mrs. O'Brien nodded and lowered the cloth. "Please do come back with the girls this evening. We start around eight."

Zellie nodded, caught off guard. Mrs. Gird would never approve—she would forbid it, Zellie was almost sure. "Thank you," Zellie said aloud.

Mrs. O'Brien smiled and waved the dripping cloth. "Thank *you*. I truly feel better. It's a small miracle."

Zellie smiled back at her and turned for the door just as it opened. A heavyset woman wearing a black wool coat came in. She glanced at Zellie and hesitated, meeting Mrs. O'Brien's eyes without saying anything at all.

Mrs. O'Brien smiled. "I haven't seen any of the girls yet, but—"

"I just want to leave you this," the woman interrupted. "You can give it to our friends when they come tonight." She held out a thin stack of paper.

Mrs. O'Brien nodded. "Thank you."

"It's two other houses. They thought it'd be easiest if one of us brought it to you here."

"I will deliver it safely," Mrs. O'Brien said.

The woman nodded without smiling and turned abruptly. As she went out, Mrs. O'Brien sighed. Zellie looked back at her and caught a glimpse of the paper as Mrs. O'Brien carried it back behind the counter and put it in a drawer.

It looked like a list.

A list of names.

CHAPTER FOUR

Zellie walked slowly down Central Street. The snow in the road worked its way further into her shoes with every step. It pressed against her damp stockings and they froze, rubbing her cold skin as she walked.

Zellie glanced back at the little millinery shop. It had been so warm inside. She wanted to go back, to talk to Mrs. O'Brien about Grandmamma. She would understand, Zellie was sure. Mrs. O'Brien had a very kind face.

"Be careful," Zellie told herself aloud. She knew what Grandmamma thought of a certain kind of white woman who tripped over her fancy skirts to help Negro people.

"They feel sorry for Negroes," Zellie scolded herself. "And they honestly do hate slavery . . . but none of that means Mrs. O'Brien really cares one little whit about *me*."

Zellie stepped up her pace a little, hugging herself to keep her tattered coat closed against the chill.

She could smell boiling coffee from the stage station and she wished she could buy a cup—not for the bitter black coffee, but for the sugar and the steam tickling her nose.

"You can't afford to buy *steam,*" she said aloud. Then she noticed a woman walking the other direction glancing her way and knew she had said it louder than she had meant to.

She lowered her eyes and walked a little faster, her cheeks heating up. Talking out loud might be a bad habit now that she was living in a crowded house in a town instead of on a lonely farm.

"It's not bad. You didn't have any bad habits, Grandmamma," Zellie whispered a second later, feeling guilty. She looked upward. Her throat ached with a rush of sadness and she bit at her lip, hard.

If people saw her talking to herself, then bursting into tears, they would assume she was in trouble and they'd want to know what was wrong. And she didn't want to talk to strangers about this.

Zellie swallowed. All she wanted was to have her grandmother back. She wanted to come home from her hoeing work on Ziebert's farm and see the chimney spouting supper-smoke. She longed to hear Grandmamma humming as she cooked.

Just keep walking, Zellie told herself silently. She pulled in a long breath. She had told herself to keep walking all the way from Billerica. If it hadn't been wintertime, she would have walked all the way to Boston, or maybe Philadelphia. Since it was winter, she'd made it this far at least. What else could she do?

Zellie bit her lower lip again until the tears subsided. Then she lifted her head as she came closer to the canal. The dark water flowed in the smooth channel. There was thin ice along the sides, but the center was swift enough to keep the water from freezing.

A snow-muted cadence of galloping hooves made her turn. A stagecoach was coming up Central Street, heading for the station, sagging under the weight of its passengers. It swayed as the driver hauled on the reins, bringing the six-horse hitch down to a trot before he turned the corner and stopped in front of the stage office.

Walking more slowly, Zellie watched the coach pass. Then she slowed again to get a good look as the passengers got out, straightening their cramped legs. A tall man and the woman with him were wearing the oddest coats. Zellie stared. Fur. The coats were both made out of some kind of fur. Were they from the west somewhere? Maybe the man was a trapper—one of the mountain men she had read about.

Zellie blinked. No. The man wore a top hat and the woman's dress, showing from beneath the coat's hem, was a fine, smooth wool, the color of red roses.

Zellie crossed the road to see better. The people were both dark haired, with light eyes. As she got closer she could hear them talking. It took her a second to realize that they weren't speaking English.

Their words tumbled out so close together that it seemed to Zellie that they were not pausing often enough to breathe.

What was it? French? German? Zellie had no idea. She had never actually heard a language besides her own. Or not more than a word or two from some old farmer.

Trying not to stare, Zellie slowed until she was barely sauntering. Then she stopped and knelt, pretending to fix a shoe button.

Other passengers were making their way out of the coach now. One was a pale-faced girl with reddish hair. She looked around, her eyes wide.

Still talking fast in his own language, the tall man pointed at the spires of St. Anne's church, then at the red brick buildings farther up the canal.

A little sound of dismay from the girl turned Zellie's gaze away from the tall man. The driver was taking down the trunks and cases. For a moment, Zellie thought he had damaged the girl's luggage and she was upset. But then she turned away and stared out at the farms across the river. A cow lowed again and the girl's right hand flew up to cover her mouth.

The tall man was still talking and Zellie stared at him for a moment. How odd it was to hear a person speaking and not be able to understand anything he said.

Then Zellie looked back at the girl. She was talking to the driver in a low voice. He dropped a case to the ground, then turned and gestured up Central Street, past the little bridge that ran across the canal.

The girl shouldered a cloth sack and started off, trudging so slowly, with her head bent low, that for a moment Zellie wondered if the bag was too heavy for her to carry. But she didn't set it down nor did she stop. Clumping along, she turned into the street a little ways ahead of Zellie.

Zellie stood quickly, then was embarrassed when she realized the tall man was looking at her. She had been staring rudely at them all, she knew, but now that he was looking at her, she felt her face heat up and she averted her eyes and began to walk.

Zellie walked fast. When she overtook the red-headed girl, she crossed the road and kept her head down except to nod politely. Her frozen stockings grated at her feet and all she wanted was to get back to the boardinghouse.

"Can you give me directions?" the girl asked as Zellie started to turn up Merrimack Street.

"I've been here only four days," Zellie said, apologetically.

The girl looked like she was about to burst into

tears. "You could just come with me," Zellie said. "Mrs. Gird will know how to direct you."

The girl lifted her chin a little. "Mrs. Gird?"

Zellie nodded. "The woman I work for."

"She has a boardinghouse?"

Zellie nodded again.

"That's who I was supposed to find," the girl said breathlessly. "Mrs. Gird's place for Merrimack Mills— that's where I am to stay!"

She sounded so relieved that Zellie smiled.

"What's she like?" the girl asked. Then she shook her head. "I apologize. My name is Plumy Clay."

"And I am Zellie Blake," Zellie told her.

They smiled at each other again.

"I am so frightened," Plumy said as they waded through the snow in front of St. Anne's.

Zellie nodded without saying anything. She was scared, too, but Plumy's quavering voice worried her. She didn't want to start her crying.

"Do you work in the mills?" Plumy asked, switching the bag from one shoulder to the other.

Zellie shook her head. "There aren't any Negroes in the mills, I don't think. I would if I could."

Plumy shook her head sorrowfully. "I would rather be home than here. If I could give you my job and scurry right back to the farm, I surely would."

Zellie glanced at Plumy from the corner of her eye. This pale girl had a voice like a squeaking mouse.

She sounded so upset, so timid, that Zellie hated to take her to someone as unkind as Mrs. Gird.

"Oh, I mean it," Plumy assured her as though Zellie had argued the point. "The only reason I have had to come is that my brother is hurt. He can't work off the farm this year and last year's crops were lean. So I have to." She lowered her head to stare at the snowy road again.

"This way," Zellie said, gesturing. Plumy fell into step beside her as she led the way across the street, then into the open space in front of the print works. "It's over there," Zellie told her, pointing.

"I've never been in a three-storied building," Plumy said, glancing around. "All these buildings seem too big to me. They make me feel so small." She shifted her bag again. "Like an ant," she added and her high voice sounded fainter with each word.

Zellie nodded. "I feel like that, but I hope I can get used to it."

Plumy gave her a quick smile and the fear in the girl's eyes amazed Zellie. "Wouldn't you rather just be back home?"

Zellie nodded, but didn't say anything.

"Where are you from?" Plumy asked.

"Billerica," Zellie told her.

Plumy nodded. "I come from Hingham. It's nearly fifty miles."

Zellie nodded sympathetically. She had no idea

where Hingham was or how to get there, but Plumy was staring into her face, her eyes red from travel or weeping.

"That couple was from Italy," Plumy said breathlessly as they crossed behind the print works and headed for the boarding house. "His coat was of beaver fur. Hers was made from fox fur. Beautiful, red-gold fox fur. Did you see it?"

"I wondered what it was," Zellie said. Then she glanced up and saw Mrs. Gird standing on the back stoop, her hands on her hips.

"Who is that?" Plumy asked. "Is that Mrs. Gird?" Her voice was tremulous again.

Zellie nodded unhappily. "That's her."

CHAPTER FIVE

"What in the world took you so long?" Mrs. Gird called across the snowy yard.

Zellie didn't know what to say, so she said nothing at all and walked faster. She didn't want Mrs. Gird to think she had dawdled along the way.

"And who are you?" Mrs. Gird demanded, staring at Plumy.

The pale girl lowered her head and her eyes and stared at the ground. "Plumy Clay, Ma'am."

Mrs. Gird nodded, but Zellie was sure that Plumy didn't see her. Mrs. Gird must have realized it, too, because she reached out and took Plumy's chin in her work-roughened hand and lifted her head. "They give me a list most weeks," Mrs. Gird said. "I don't recall a Plumy on my list. Are you sure you are in the right house?"

"The agent said . . ." Plumy's eyes welled with tears.

Mrs. Gird clucked impatiently. "The agents don't

always let me know," she said. "Hold your cloudburst till we find out."

Mrs. Gird shook her head and turned to Zellie. "You deliver the buttons?"

Zellie nodded. "Mrs. O'Brien sends her kind regards," she said.

Mrs. Gird did not smile. "*Mrs.?* Indeed not. She is *Miss* O'Brien. Never married, that one. No man wanted to deal with that iron will of hers."

Zellie blinked. She had known only one other woman who hadn't ever married—her Auntie Persis. But Mrs. . . . *Miss* O'Brien had seemed soft and sweet to her—not strong willed in any way that would put suitors off. Not like Auntie Persis was, at any rate.

"Well, come in, come in," Mrs. Gird was saying. "Our girls will be trouping home any time now."

"What shall I do?" Plumy asked in her wavering, quiet voice.

Mrs. Gird glanced at her. "Is that all you brought with you?"

Plumy nodded, and her cheeks went deep red. "It is, Ma'am."

Zellie felt terrible for her. "I don't have even that much," she whispered once Mrs. Gird had clumped up the steps and into the house.

Plumy shot her a tiny smile, then shook her head. "I am so scared."

"You'll get used to it," Zellie told her.

"Move along!" Mrs. Gird called and they hurried inside.

"Show her to her room," Mrs. Gird told Zellie. "First floor, one door past the storeroom, left side. The bed nearest the door has a space. Then hurry back."

Zellie nodded and walked a little faster so Plumy could fall in behind her. Her feet felt like blocks of wood. Frozen wood.

"Are the girls nice?" Plumy asked as Zellie led her down the long hallway.

Zellie glanced back at her. "I suppose. They seem to like each other well enough."

Plumy flushed deep red again. "That's a silly question, I know. I am just . . . shy." She sighed.

Zellie took a deep breath and faced front, hoping that Plumy could find her way fairly quickly here in Lowell. She was going to wear down everyone around her if she didn't. "You don't seem all that shy," she said aloud.

"I am, though," Plumy insisted from behind her.

"Here's the room," Zellie told her, pointing at the door.

Plumy opened the door slowly, gasping once she could see inside. "It's so nice," she whispered. "So clean and nice and all."

Zellie nodded. "Two to a bed."

Plumy set her bag down on the bed, then

snatched it up and ran her hand over the white spread, smiling in relief when she saw that she hadn't soiled it. "Who's my partner?"

Zellie shrugged. "I only know one or two of the girls by name," she said, thinking about the mysterious note signed "Lydia." "Like I said, I have only been here—"

"A few days," Plumy finished for her. "I am so sorry, you did tell me that." She set her bag on the bed again, then lifted it and moved it to the floor.

"May I use that bureau?" she asked, pointing at a chest of drawers close to the footboard.

Zellie shrugged, then nodded. "I think so. It's the one closest to your bed." She glanced back down the hall. "I better go."

Plumy nodded, fidgeting. "Thank you for showing me here," she said. "I am most grateful."

"You're welcome," Zellie said, backing away. It felt funny to leave this timid girl alone, as if she were walking off from a child young enough to get into trouble without someone watching. But that was silly. Plumy looked fourteen or fifteen. And she had come all the way on the stagecoach alone.

"I'll just walk back with you," Plumy said. "Surely Mrs. Gird won't mind."

Zellie hesitated. She had no idea what Mrs. Gird would mind or not mind.

"I can help," Plumy added.

Zellie shrugged. "You will have to talk to Mrs. Gird about it," she said.

Plumy sighed. "I know. Is she ever nice?"

Zellie hesitated again. Then she shook her head. "Not yet. Not really."

Plumy sighed once more and her face sank back into the pale, frozen expression Zellie had seen at the stage stop. "Come on," she said, and walked away fast, before the girl could heave another long, sad sigh.

Back in the kitchen, Zellie stirred the stew Mrs. Gird had cooked for the girls' dinner while Plumy laid the tables.

Zellie began to feel a little better as she warmed up. The clinking of the plateware and the water cups was pleasant enough. The heat from the hearth was heaven itself. Zellie took her shoes off and laid them close to the coals, the holey soles faced upward to dry. Then she stood flat-footed on the warm stone to dry her soaked stockings.

Zellie could see two big Dutch ovens buried in the ashes, their raised rims holding mounds of hot ashes like thick, gray winter hats.

Zellie inhaled. Corn bread, she was almost sure. And the stew had chunks of beef floating around in it along with carrots and potatoes and celeriac. She leaned forward again to stir in slow circles, careful not to drop the long-handled spoon into the pot. As she worked, the fire flared up a little in front of the pot and she felt it singe the downy hair from her forearms.

Grandmamma had never had a single hair on her arms and half the time her eyelashes were burnt as well. She had always laughed about it. "A woman with all her lashes isn't doing enough cooking," Zellie murmured to herself, reciting Grandmamma's words.

It sounded odd in her own high, girlish voice. Grandmamma had had a rich deep voice that boomed out in the hymns on Sundays.

"Zellie!" Mrs. Gird called.

Startled, Zellie nearly dropped the spoon, then caught herself and managed to hang it on its hook and wipe her eyes before she turned around. "Yes, Ma'am?"

"Are you strong enough to get those ovens out of the ashes?"

Zellie nodded slowly. "I think so."

"I'll help her," Plumy volunteered and Zellie was grateful. The iron pots were bigger than any she had ever handled and like all Dutch ovens, they were made of thick cast iron.

"Where are the pot rags?" Plumy asked as she walked closer, making her way around the tables.

Zellie pointed and Plumy veered off, then came back with wads of old red flannel padding her hands.

Zellie slipped her shoes back on. They weren't dry, but they were warm and it felt wonderful. Then she wrapped her cloths tightly around her own hands.

They bent down together. "I'll count three," Zellie said.

Plumy made a little sound of agreement and Zellie grasped the handle on her end of the Dutch oven. The coals on the lid were still glowing and Zellie felt her face stinging from the heat. She counted steadily and on three, they swung the pot up onto the hearth, then both stepped back. Plumy's face was as red as beets.

"Just a second," she said, taking a deep breath. Then she nodded. "Ready."

Zellie counted again and they hoisted the second Dutch oven a few inches in the air, stepping backward together to place it on the hearth next to the first one.

"Let them sit," Mrs. Gird instructed, coming toward them. "Leave the lids until the last minute. I like to serve it hot."

Zellie's mouth began to water. One good thing about this boardinghouse was the food. Mrs. Gird might be grumpy, but she could cook.

"Not as good as you, Grandmamma," Zellie said quietly, glancing upward.

Plumy turned. "Pardon me?"

"Nothing," Zellie said, embarrassed.

Just then she heard the mill girls coming. It was

an odd sound, a mixture of footsteps and voices that swept across the snowy yard.

"There's so many of them," Plumy said as the back door opened and the long line of girls could be seen. They all wiped their feet, their steamy breath disappearing as they came inside.

"We have a new girl," Mrs. Gird shouted over the friendly chatter. Silence fell in the room. "Plumy . . ." She hesitated and it was obvious that she had forgotten Plumy's surname.

Zellie glanced at Plumy. Her cheeks had gone red and she was looking at her feet. Mrs. Gird cleared her throat impatiently.

"Her name is Plumy Clay," Zellie said clearly, filling the awkward silence. "She came from Hingham on the stage."

The silence closed down again and Plumy made a tiny sound, like a cornered animal.

"There was a couple all the way from Italy on the stage," Zellie said, a little louder. "The woman had on a fox-fur coat the color of autumn leaves and sunset, mixed."

That worked. The girls began to murmur, talking about fur coats and Italians, glancing enviously at Plumy as they found their places along the long table.

"Let's sit at this end," Plumy whispered.

Zellie shook her head. "Mrs. Gird won't let me sit at the tables."

Plumy blushed again, a painful red that made her light reddish hair look like blanched barley straw. "I'm sorry. I appreciate what you did for me. Everything," she added. "I mean walking me home and talking to me and not making fun of me." She sounded close to tears again.

Zellie wanted to reach out and pat Plumy's hand, but she didn't. Mrs. Gird might see her.

"Find a seat," Mrs. Gird called to Plumy. "Dinner break is only a half hour and these girls need to eat."

Plumy caught Zellie's eye once more, then headed for the tables, her head down like a shamed pup.

Zellie went to the sideboard and got a stack of bowls. The girls pulled off their coats, draping them over the backs of their chairs, then they began to line up.

It was getting easier for Zellie. The first day or two she had been terrified of slopping soup or causing one of the girls to drop her bowl—or going too slow.

"Mmmm, it looks good," the first girl in line said. She had long brown hair, done up in a tight bun like all the others.

"Hurry, please," the girl behind her pleaded.

"Oh, be patient," the first girl teased, pretending to scold even though she was smiling.

"Lydia," the second one said, pouting. "You weavers have it easy up there, with just the two looms this week, and half your time spent getting girls to sign the—"

"Hush!" Lydia said, a little too loudly. Then she glanced at Zellie.

Zellie tried hard to keep her face perfectly bland. Was there another Lydia in the house? Or was this the one? Zellie saw Mrs. Gird glaring at her and she hurried to fill the first bowl. She handed it to Lydia carefully.

"Thank you, Zellie," Lydia said politely.

Zellie stared at her, startled. When had Lydia learned *her* name? Mrs. Gird had not bothered to introduce her to any of the girls. "You're welcome," Zellie managed, but it took her a few seconds and Lydia had already started away. Still, Lydia heard her. She smiled over her shoulder, then walked on to her table.

"We're having a mathematics evening class," the next girl was saying. "They want to use Colburn's Arithmetic for the text, so we are going to share the cost."

She turned to face Zellie long enough to take her bowl, then stepped aside, still talking to her friend.

The conversations in the line were often about night classes and Zellie wanted to ask if she could attend, but she knew Mrs. Gird wouldn't like her talking to the girls—or planning to spend time with them in the evenings.

Mrs. Gird cut up the corn bread and served it on

platters that the girls passed around. She put out jam and butter, then Zellie served the milk.

Plumy was sitting toward the back. She smiled at Zellie when she set the milk pitcher and cups on the table. "They are going to take me to the mill and show me around the different workrooms after dinner," she said happily.

Zellie smiled back, glad that Plumy had chanced to sit by particularly friendly girls. Or maybe they just felt sorry for her.

It didn't really matter which, Zellie thought as she started back for more milk. Plumy was happy.

By the time Zellie got to the last table, some of the girls at the front of the room were standing up to go.

They carried their dirty dishes to the sideboard and stacked them neatly, spoons in the basin and bowls to one side.

"Run to the storeroom and fetch the slops bucket," Mrs. Gird said as the girls were putting on their coats.

Zellie nodded. She wouldn't be able to scrape the bowls until they were gone. There was no real hurry except that she was hungry. And she wouldn't get to eat until all the work was done and the kitchen put back in order.

Zellie eased her way through the crowd of chatting girls and headed up the hallway. She longed to eat before she cleaned up—being out in the cold air had made her hungry—but she knew Mrs. Gird would never let her. It seemed unfair. But it would be foolish to tell Mrs. Gird that, Zellie knew.

Reaching out for the storeroom door, Zellie thought about just sneaking off to go to Miss O'Brien's that evening. It could cause trouble. What would Mrs. Gird do if she noticed? Even if Zellie came home with all kinds of snippets she had overheard—or even some real explanation of the girls' secrets, Mrs. Gird would be angry if she went without permission.

"I have no choice," she said to herself as she pulled the door open. "I will have to tell Mrs. Gird."

Then she stopped and stared. Lydia and two other girls were in the storeroom—and they were all looking at her, their eyes wide.

CHAPTER SIX

Zellie blinked.

"You can't tell her!" Lydia said in a low voice.

"Please . . ." A girl with jet-black hair pleaded.

"If they stop us this time, we might never manage to get the girls together again."

"How did you find out?" Lydia asked sharply, her eyes narrowed.

Zellie's heart was pounding. They were reacting to what she had been saying to herself as she walked in, but she had no idea what they were really talking about. But she was sure it had something to do with whatever Mrs. Gird had wanted her to listen for. And if she *could* find out, Mrs. Gird had said she could stay at least until spring.

"Everyone has been whispering," Zellie answered carefully, watching Lydia's face.

Lydia glanced at the ceiling, then down again. "Grand. And they will spoil it for us all. Do they think it is a game?"

Her voice was tight and angry and she was looking straight at Zellie.

"Zellie?" a tremulous voice asked from the hallway. "Are you in there?"

Lydia and the others went still again. From the corner of her eye, Zellie saw Lydia tuck a piece of folded paper beneath a laundry bag. Then she patted at her hair and yawned as Plumy came in.

"You're the new girl, aren't you?" Lydia asked.

Plumy blushed a deep shade of rose and nodded. Then she faced Zellie. "I asked Mrs. Gird if I should dish up your stew and corn bread and she told me you couldn't eat until after the kitchen is clean."

Zellie nodded, trying to keep an eye on Lydia without being obvious about it. What was on that paper? More names? Another note like the one in her room?

"So I brought you this," Plumy said. She pulled a folded napkin from behind her back and handed it to Zellie. The delicious smell of warm corn bread tickled Zellie's nose.

"Thank you," she said, and she meant it.

Lydia stepped toward the door, the other two girls following like chicks behind a hen.

"Zellie," Lydia said just as she stepped out. "Please, don't say a word to anyone! I'll explain everything this evening."

Plumy looked curious. "What was all that about?"

Zellie shrugged. "I think they were gossiping in here when I came in," she said.

Plumy smiled. "I am sure they get disagreeable from being so crowded all the time." She looked at Zellie, her eyes shiny with tears. "At home I slept with my baby sister." She wiped at her eyes. "Just the two of us in our little room."

Zellie nodded. "I had my own little bed-closet in Grandmamma's house. I sleep by the hearth here," she told Plumy.

Plumy's eyes widened. "Without a bed?"

Zellie started to say something, then closed her mouth. She had no business trusting Plumy with her opinions. It was likely that the only reason this girl had talked to her at all was because she had no one else to talk to . . . yet. And maybe Plumy would tell Mrs. Gird that she had been complaining.

Zellie ate the corn bread, chewing fast. Mrs. Gird would be wondering where she was, she was sure. "Thank you," she said to Plumy as she dusted the last tiny crumbs from her hands. "I get terribly hungry before she lets me eat—and it's the same after supper."

"That's awful." Plumy sighed. "I'll save you something every meal."

Her gaze was so open and direct that Zellie had to smile. This girl seemed honest and kind. "You should eat your own food, Plumy."

"I don't ever eat very much," Plumy told her as they walked down the hall together.

"Are you coming, Plumy?" A girl called from the kitchen door. "We have to get back, or Mr. Teller will scold us."

Plumy shot Zellie a quick smile. "I'll tell you all about the weaving room tonight."

Zellie managed to smile back. Plumy might be silly, but she was so nice that it was impossible not to like her a little. "See you this evening," Zellie said.

Plumy ran down the hall. Turning to wave at Zellie, she disappeared with the other mill girls.

"Let's get started," Mrs. Gird said as Zellie set the slops bucket at one end of the drainboard.

Zellie pulled in a long breath, grateful for Plumy's bit of corn bread. It would be at least an hour before she finished washing the dishes and sweeping the floors.

Mrs. Gird brought a steaming pot of water from the hearth and poured it into the basin.

Most of the girls had eaten all their food, but some had not, and there were bits of vegetables and meat stuck to the sides of all the bowls. Zellie used a pot scraper on the ones with the most garbage, and a wooden butter paddle on the rest.

The slops bucket was close to full when she finished.

"Take it out back," Mrs. Gird said, walking past.

Zellie pulled on her coat and took the egg basket from its hook. With the heavy slops bucket in one hand and the empty basket in the other, she walked the path leading around to the back of the building.

The chickens were happy to see her. They clucked and scratched at the scraps as she searched the nest boxes for eggs.

As she set the eggs carefully in the basket, Zellie thought about the farms around Billerica. They all had raised one or two hogs a year—at least. With this much cooking and so many eating, there was enough in the bucket every morning to feed a hog or two, but none of the boardinghouses in Lowell seemed to keep them.

It seemed silly to Zellie, but the boardinghouse keepers appeared to be content to leave the hog raising to the farmers who lived all around Lowell, then pay dearly for their pork and ham.

"Hurry along," Mrs. Gird said when Zellie came in carrying the empty bucket in one hand and the egg basket in the other.

Zellie set the basket down carefully.

"I'll want you to meet the laundry wagon out front, then there are the washrooms," Mrs. Gird was saying. "Then I have another errand for you to run."

Zellie sighed and faced the steaming basin of dishwater.

Nearly an hour later, she was sweeping the last

of the crumbs out the back door, then off the porch.

"Hurry, Zellie!" Mrs. Gird said from the doorway. Startled, Zellie turned around.

"Eat your dinner and be quick about it. You need to get the laundry bags out front before Mrs. Varner's son comes. Every time he has to wait, I get back a ruined sheet. I think she switches new for old sometimes."

Zellie nodded. "Yes, Ma'am."

She watched Mrs. Gird walk out of the kitchen, turning to the right, heading back toward her room. Mrs. Gird seemed to think that everyone was dishonest.

"Like finds like," she said aloud, echoing another of her grandmother's sayings. She wasn't quite sure what it meant, but it had something to do with people who were always suspicious being the ones you should be suspicious of.

Zellie shook her head. She didn't really think that Mrs. Gird was dishonest; just selfish. If she could make things go her way, she would.

Grandmamma had been the opposite. She had given to everyone who ever needed anything. She had taken in every passerby, fed strangers at their hearth and not one had ever done them even small harm. Grandmamma had trusted them all.

Zellie turned toward the hearth. The fire had burnt down, but the heavy, iron cauldron had kept the stew warm. She got her dish from the cracker box and filled it to the brim, then sat at one of the tables to eat.

She rose only once, to get seconds, then came back and kept her mind on her food, chewing as fast as she could. She tipped up the bowl to drink the last dregs of the stew.

Even so, she had barely finished when Mrs. Gird came striding back into the kitchen.

"Come to the storeroom, Zellie," she said curtly and turned on her heel.

Zellie ran a few steps to catch up, then suddenly remembered the piece of paper that Lydia had slid beneath the laundry sack. What in the world was it that she was hiding it like that?

Zellie sighed. Maybe the paper would tell her what Mrs. Gird wanted to know. She should probably go get it and read it to find out. But it felt wrong to read it, no matter what Lydia was up to.

"You need this position," she whispered aloud.

Lydia had hidden the paper for a reason, Zellie knew, innocent or sly. But why would she leave it in the storeroom on laundry day? That seemed just plain silly.

As soon as she wondered, Zellie knew the answer. Lydia didn't know that laundry day had been moved from Monday to Thursday. She had assumed no one would move the laundry bags for days.

"I can manage this," Zellie said as they came to the door.

"I'll help," Mrs. Gird said. "Just to hurry it along. Like I said, he hates to wait."

Zellie turned, stepping backward to stand in front of the bag beneath which Lydia had placed the paper.

Mrs. Gird picked up one of the heavy sacks and started out of the room with it.

Zellie bent over and picked up the sack, swinging it to one side and setting it down again. The paper lay there, creased and flattened by the weight of the bag.

"Come on!" Mrs. Gird called from the hallway. Zellie shoved the paper inside her bodice and hoisted the bag up over her shoulder. Then she walked quickly to catch up with Mrs. Gird.

Crossing the snowy yard wet Zellie's stockings again. She sighed, then forced herself to forget about the cold. It would do her no good to dwell on it. There was nothing she could do about it until she had saved enough money for new shoes.

"Which means you had better keep this position," she whispered to herself, speeding up her step.

Mrs. Gird carried one more bag, then left Zellie to haul the rest. There were four more bags of linens and two more of rags and towels and tablecloths. The bags were heavy, but Zellie didn't allow herself to slow down until they were all outside. Just as she brought out the last one, the wagon came around the corner.

"Good girl," Mrs. Gird said as Zellie came in the back door.

Zellie risked a smile.

Mrs. Gird didn't smile back, but at least she didn't frown. "Clean the girls' washrooms on each floor, then come back down and do the little parlor."

CHAPTER SEVEN

Zellie got the vinegar water and the lye soap out of the storeroom cupboard, then reached into the bin for some rough, stout rags. She clomped up the stairs, trying not to think about how far above the solid sweet earth she was getting with every step.

She was fine until she stepped out onto the third-floor landing and caught a glimpse out the window. She took a deep breath and turned away from the dizzying view.

In the washroom she wiped the little round mirror with vinegar water, then shined up the glass. She carried the brownish wash water down and flung it out the back door.

Using the big kitchen basin and hot water from the kettle, she washed out the sticky bits of soap from the wide glass wash bowl, wiped it out, and took it back upstairs. This time, she refused to let the window draw her gaze.

As she worked Zellie kept her ears open, expecting

Mrs. Gird to come up to check on her. But she didn't. So once the third-floor washroom was clean, Zellie set down her rag and reached inside her bodice.

The piece of paper opened flat to reveal only five lines of writing. Zellie stared at it.

Weaving room—everyone but three Doffers—left out for their age. Perhaps they will join us anyway.
Spinners—all but four.
Drawing-in girls—six say they will come, the others won't say yet, but I so hope they will.

Zellie shook her head, puzzled. Maybe, Zellie thought, folding the paper back up, it was just some kind of get-together. Maybe something for church. If it hadn't been winter, she would have thought Lydia might be organizing a church picnic.

She slipped the paper back in her bodice, then began gathering up her rags and the jar of vinegar water. Or maybe someone *was* getting married. Maybe Lydia was organizing the guests?

Zellie frowned and went down the stairs. Cleaning the second-floor washroom, Zellie tried hard to figure it out. She was curious and for a second, she thought about going back upstairs and reading the paper inside Lydia's writing box again. But she knew she wouldn't.

Grandmamma had always thought snooping was

almost like stealing, and Zellie agreed with that. She'd hate for anyone to read her diary. Whatever Lydia was planning, it was her own business.

"But Mrs. Gird wants to know," Zellie murmured. "And she expects me to find out for her." She shook her head. She had work to finish; when she was done, then she would think about what she should do or not do with the paper. She wished that her position didn't depend on snooping. But she knew it just might.

The first-floor washroom took a little more time. It got more use. Girls in the parlor and the kitchen late at night used it to wash their faces before bed. Half the house used it for a quick hand-wash after breakfast. Zellie hurried along, rubbing hard at the woodwork and polishing the little mirror to a flawless shine.

Finishing up, Zellie realized something that made her feel foolish, then nervous. Lydia would certainly notice that the bag had been moved and that her paper was gone. If she found out that Zellie had carried the bags out to the street . . .

Zellie bit at her lip. "Then she will get angry at me," she said aloud. And she knew it was true.

Lydia might notice that the papers in her writing box had been shuffled. If she did, that would be it. Lydia might tell Mrs. Gird about the writing box. And what could either one of them possibly think?

Zellie Blake   67

"That I am a snoop at best." Zellie completed the thought aloud. "Or at worst, a thief."

Zellie sighed. Not only would she lose her position if that happened, she would hardly be given a letter of recommendation. It had been difficult enough to get this job without a letter of some kind. If the boardinghouse keepers passed around a list of those not to hire, she'd *have* to leave Lowell and she had no money for a fare to Philadelphia or anywhere else.

Zellie felt her eyes ache and she marched herself down the stairs, keeping her chin high. Maybe she could just return the paper to Lydia and explain that she had seen her hide it—then had simply made sure that Mrs. Gird didn't see it.

Zellie lifted her chin even higher. What was wrong with that? Mrs. Gird didn't need to know about a party or a wedding, did she? And that was likely all it was. Mrs. Gird was suspicious by nature. She might always think there was something brewing when it was nothing at all.

Humming a lively tune to try to cheer herself up, Zellie walked into the little parlor. She stopped abruptly and wrinkled her nose. The air was stale and it smelled like dust. Mrs. Gird had not been taking care of the house as well as she could have. The rugs needed beating and no one had opened the window in a long time.

Grateful that the room was on the ground floor,

Zellie pulled the window draperies aside and looked out. The sky was clouding up. Maybe they were in for another storm. She slid the window upward. It creaked and squealed. She stepped back and inhaled big draughts of the fresh, cold air.

"I aired out just last week," Mrs. Gird said from the doorway. Zellie flinched, started.

"It smelled a little stale," Zellie said. "I thought I would let a little fresh air in. Just for a minute," she added, when she saw Mrs. Gird's frown deepen.

"The day you are paying for the firewood, you can sleep with the windows open for all I care," Mrs. Gird scolded her. "Until then, if you find them closed, leave them closed."

Zellie glanced at her, then looked away quickly. Mrs. Gird's face was pink and she was frowning hard.

"I'm sorry, Mrs. Gird," Zellie said carefully, looking down at her feet.

"Just dust and straighten in here. Then I want you to go up to Central Street again. The potatoes the grocery man delivered are soft and I can't wait until next week for him to make it right—they'll be black and rotten by then—and I need some for supper tonight." Her voice was still tense and half angry.

"Yes, Ma'am," Zellie said quietly.

As Mrs. Gird left, Zellie reached for a rag. "I am not sure I can stand working for you a second longer than I have to," she murmured.

"What? Do you need something, Zellie?" Mrs. Gird called to her.

Zellie drew in a quick breath and held it, then let it out slowly. "No, Ma'am," she called back after a few seconds.

The little drawing room was as dusty as it smelled. Zellie had to get two more clean rags before she was through. She wanted to take the settee pillows outside and beat the dust out of them, and the carpet too. But she knew that Mrs. Gird didn't want her to, at least not today. Still, that was what they needed.

"I'm finished," she told Mrs. Gird, walking into the kitchen.

"Good," Mrs. Gird said. "Wait here. I'll get the potatoes."

Zellie stood still while Mrs. Gird walked across the room and opened the pantry door. She disappeared inside it.

Zellie got her coat from the hook by the door and carried it back to the hearth and put it on. Then she turned her back to the fire, letting the tattered wool absorb the heat.

Zellie inhaled the steam that was rising from the stew pot. Onions and beef were boiling. Supper was started.

"Here," Mrs. Gird said, backing out of the pantry. She was carrying a bulging sack. "The grocer I use is only a block down from the millinery. If I had noticed these were bad this morning, you could have taken them then."

Zellie was glad Mrs. Gird hadn't noticed because she *wanted* to get outside. Walking, even carrying a heavy sack, was better than cleaning any day. "Even with holes in my shoes?" she asked herself in a whisper, then looked up sharply to see if Mrs. Gird had noticed. She hadn't. She was preoccupied with tying twine around the mouth of the potato sack.

"I want you to tell Mr. Aldritt that this is the second time in a month. If the potatoes are all going bad, he needs to throw them out, not sell them to me."

Zellie nodded, knowing she would have a very hard time repeating anything so rude to any grown man—and it'd be even harder if Mr. Aldritt was white.

"His shop is a block down from Miss O'Brien's," Mrs. Gird repeated. "You'll have to make it quicker than you did this morning, though."

Zellie nodded. "I didn't dawdle last time, I just happened to come across Plumy and—"

"Just make it quicker this time," Mrs. Gird repeated, cutting her off with a curt gesture. "I don't want to be serving supper without help tonight."

Zellie nodded and took the sack from her. It was *heavy.* She hoisted it over her left shoulder and hitched it up a little higher as she started for the back door.

"Be sure you don't dawdle!" Mrs. Gird said, her voice sharp.

"Yes, Ma'am," Zellie answered, then opened the door and went out.

The clouds were thin and high, but they had closed the vault of the sky. There was no blue at all to be seen now.

Zellie walked as fast as she could, cutting through the block by the print works again, then passing the church. Then she had to stop and set the bag down for a moment before she could go on.

Her stockings were already soaked. In warming her coat, she had warmed her shoes and now the snow was melting twice as fast against the soles of her feet.

Walking as fast as she could with the heavy sack hanging down her back, Zellie went on. She crossed the canal and hurried past the stage office. She could still smell coffee on the cold air.

Zellie set down the sack for another moment, then switched shoulders as she hoisted it back up.

Walking with shorter and shorter steps, she passed the millinery shop and kept going without looking left or right. The sack seemed to get heavier. She could feel Lydia's paper inside her bodice, rubbing at her skin through her thin chemise. But she didn't want to stop to reposition it. She just wanted to keep going.

By the time she pushed open the grocer's door and wobbled inside, her hands ached from holding onto the rough cloth. Sighing in relief, she lowered the sack to the floor.

"Girl? What are you doing there?" a man asked and Zellie looked up at him.

He was tall and broad, and his eyes were striking—nearly black. His dark moustache was as grand as the rest of him. He had grown it long, then waxed it to make the ends curl. He smelled of pomade, clear across the shop. "Mrs. Gird sent me to ask if—"

"And what is wrong this week?" he interrupted, his voice tight and irritated.

This week? Zellie took a breath. "She asked me to tell you that the potatoes were going bad."

The grocer scowled. "Let me see."

Zellie lifted the sack and carried it toward him, shuffling her feet along, barely managing to keep the bag from dragging on the ground.

"Here, I can take that," the man said, stepping toward her quickly. "It's as big as you are and twice as heavy," he added, his face thawing a little.

Zellie managed to smile at him. He didn't smile back, but he didn't scowl, either. He just undid the twine and looked down into the bag. He sniffed at the potatoes, then wrinkled his nose.

"Well, for once, she isn't just trying to get a little extra out of me. All the boardinghouse women are thrifty, but she's one of the worst pinchpennies. It'll ease things if the boardinghouse fees go up." He looked down at the sack and he felt the potatoes. "I don't know how I missed these," he said thoughtfully as he pulled one potato out and squeezed it gently. "They're all going soft at the same time this year," he added, his expression puzzled.

"That's what Mrs. Gird said," Zellie said politely. "She asked if you had more to replace them."

The man nodded. "I do, a wagonload brought in from John Simms's place this morning. He keeps everything in that cellar of his and it usually holds longer than the others."

Zellie nodded. Grandmamma had taught her about cellars.

The grocer picked up the bag of soft potatoes and disappeared through a door. When he returned, he was carrying an empty sack.

"I want to check through them to be sure." He looked at Zellie. "I am sure you don't want to carry another sack that heavy back here in the morning."

Zellie smiled at him. "I certainly appreciate you thinking about it that way, Sir."

"You like working for her?"

Zellie shrugged. "I have to work. I am on my own."

The grocer shook his head. "That's a hard road."

Zellie didn't know what else to say, so she just pretended to stare at the barrel of crackers beside her.

"Mrs. Gird is a hard woman," the grocer said. "You tell her I am glad to replace these potatoes. Maybe that will cheer her up for a while."

Zellie nearly laughed aloud. It sounded like he knew Mrs. Gird awfully well. "Thank you, Sir," she said, and smiled at him again. This time, he smiled back.

"I'm sorry you had to carry those," he said, pointing at the bag. "But I am glad you did. You are a sight easier to deal with than your employer."

He laughed aloud at his own joke, then set about sorting through a bin of potatoes that stood behind the cracker barrel.

Zellie watched him working for a moment, then began to help. He didn't object. He just moved aside a little so that she could do it more easily. With both of them checking to see that each potato was sound, they had the sack refilled in a few minutes.

Zellie stood up and rubbed her hands together, letting the dirt fall back in the bin.

"Some say less dirt and they keep longer. Others say the more soil the better."

"These all look good," Zellie said.

He nodded. "They do. Maybe Farmer Simms has the right amount of dirt in with them."

"Or maybe his cellar is deeper than the others," Zellie said, remembering what the grocer had said before.

He looked into Zellie's face. "I believe, now that

you say it, that he told me he'd dug it deeper last summer."

Zellie nodded. "My grandmother had a deep cellar in Billerica. We always had cabbage and potatoes and squash long after everyone else." Zellie could feel her eyes stinging and she turned her head aside.

The man's voice softened. "Your grannie pass on?"

Zellie nodded. "About two weeks ago."

"I am real sorry to hear that," he said.

Just as he straightened up, the bell on the shop door rang. Zellie looked up to see Miss O'Brien coming through the door. "Hello, Zellie," she said.

Zellie smiled. "Mrs. Gird sent me for potatoes." She saw the grocer cast her a grateful glance for not mentioning anything about the rotten ones.

"Have you got a moment to stop by my shop when you are finished here?" Miss O'Brien asked.

Zellie hesitated. "I shouldn't. Mrs. Gird said for me to hurry."

Miss O'Brien nodded pleasantly. "I only want to ask a small favor. It won't take but a moment."

Zellie nodded, and watched Miss O'Brien smile as she turned back toward the door. It took her a moment to realize that Miss O'Brien hadn't come into the grocery to buy anything.

"She must have seen me go past," she said aloud.

The grocer nodded, assuming she had spoken to

him. Then he got a length of twine and tied the top of the sack.

"Apologize to Mrs. Gird for me," he said wryly.

Zellie kept her face very serious. "I will, Sir," she said.

Back out on the street, she started toward the millinery shop, feeling uneasy. Mrs. Gird would be angry if she took too long.

CHAPTER EIGHT

"Oh, thank you," Miss O'Brien said the moment Zellie eased herself—and the heavy sack of potatoes—through the narrow door. "I actually have a favor to ask."

Zellie nodded. She started to make a polite reply, then decided to tell the truth. "I am happy to help you any time I can, Mrs. O'Brien," she said. "But Mrs. Gird told me to hurry back."

"Please call me Miss O'Brien," the old woman said in her calm, quiet voice. "I should have corrected you this morning, but I assume Bertha Gird set you straight." She smiled, a tiny upward curving of her lips.

Zellie nodded carefully. "She did. I forgot."

"Well certainly most women my age have been married and if there's no husband around, everyone assumes he's simply passed on. But I never did marry."

"My Auntie Persis says it takes a grand husband to be better than none," Zellie blurted out.

Miss O'Brien smiled, wider this time, her eyes twinkling. "I guess that's about how I always saw it."

She sighed. "And I just never fell in love. I refused to marry for a lesser reason."

Zellie nodded. It made perfect sense to her. It seemed like half the women who had come to talk and gossip with Auntie Persis and Grandmamma had complained about their husbands—sometimes bitterly.

"The laws make my life difficult, though," Miss O'Brien said sadly. "My brother has to handle all my money. The bankers won't let me manage my own accounts. But I think these mill girls are changing all that. They get paid here and their men folk are all back on the farm. They will soon have to handle their own money." Her face brightened. "It's one of my customers I need help with, Zellie," she said.

"My help?" Zellie asked, puzzled.

Miss O'Brien smiled. "Yes. It's Mrs. Thissel, the wife of the mill agent. She's coming in this evening to pick up a hat and I've not been able to finish it." She gestured out the window. "It's the clouds. It gets so dim in here that I can't see to work. Even a good astral lamp isn't enough anymore."

"I could come back tomorrow and—"

"But I have to have her out of here for the girls' meeting tonight," Miss O'Brien said. She looked upset. "It's the *mill agent's* wife, Zellie."

Zellie couldn't see why one client coming when the meeting was going on would make that much difference, but Miss O'Brien surely seemed to think it would. Zellie fiddled with the top of the sack. "What do you need me to do?"

"It's just a little stitching. To fasten down the silk roses." As she spoke, she turned and went into the back room. When she came back, she was carrying a beautiful hat, the felt the color of doves. "Are your hands clean?" she asked.

Zellie shook her head. "No. I went through fifty pounds of potatoes and I—"

"Come wash, then," Miss O'Brien said. "Set that sack down, it's about to pull you over, anyway."

Zellie let the sack slide gently to the floor and followed Miss O'Brien into the back of the shop. She looked around, surprised. The back room was *big*. There were several tables and chairs were lined up along the walls.

"There," Miss O'Brien said, pointing.

Zellie saw a washstand. The water was cold but clean. The soap smelled of lavender and it didn't burn her skin. She carefully used the towel. It had roses embroidered on it. She refolded it. She had never in her whole life used anything so pretty to dry her hands.

"It isn't much work. See?" Miss O'Brien said as Zellie turned.

Zellie looked at the hat. Miss O'Brien held it

close to the oil lamp so Zellie could see the perfect stitching that was already there, tacking down a glossy red ribbon and an ostrich plume.

"The roses go here," Miss O'Brien said, "and here." She held them in place with her fingertips. "See how it's done from the back?"

Zellie took the hat from her, feeling nervous and shy. "Grandmamma said I was no genius with a needle," she said. "I haven't practiced for the past few months and I—"

"It's simple," Miss O'Brien said, interrupting her in a gentle voice. "About six stitches each. Here." She handed the needle and thread to Zellie. "Can you pass the thread through the eye?"

Zellie nodded. That much she absolutely knew how to do. In seconds she had threaded the needle and tied a tiny knot at the end of the thread. It was good thread, she could tell—pure linen and very strong.

"Make the stitches as small as you can," Miss O'Brien cautioned her. "Straight across the stems, like railroad ties or ladder rungs." She did a pantomime in the air.

Zellie almost smiled. That was such a clever way of putting it that she understood instantly what she was supposed to do. Carefully poking the needle through the heavy felt of the hat, she managed to make very straight stitches.

"Perfect," Miss O'Brien said, tugging at the roses

to make sure they were secure. "Zellie, you have saved us. I do hope you will come tonight."

Zellie smiled.

"A number of the girls from your house will be here. Lydia Sparks will come, and Andella Franner and Abigale—do you know any of the girls yet?"

Zellie shook her head, not wanting to think about Lydia and the paper inside her bodice—and not wanting to explain Mrs. Gird's order not to be too friendly with the girls. "Not really," she said vaguely.

Miss O'Brien shook her head. "On Sundays after church you will get to know them better. You won't work on Sundays, will you?"

Zellie shrugged. "Probably. She has me cleaning and helping with meals. Maybe not, if her church forbids it."

"Bertha Gird is Episcopalian," Miss O'Brien said, arching her brows. "Not that she goes to service very often."

As she stepped back, Zellie felt the scratchy edge of the folded paper through her chemise. For an instant, she thought about giving it to Miss O'Brien to give to Lydia, then she decided against it.

She had no idea if Lydia was close to Miss O'Brien or not. What if Miss O'Brien wasn't supposed to know about the celebration or the wedding or whatever in the world it was that the girls were planning? Zellie knew she should try to find out so she could tell Mrs. Gird and keep her position at the boardinghouse. But this felt wrong. She had no idea how well Lydia knew Miss O'Brien—or if the whispering was about anything Lydia intended to keep a secret.

They probably just didn't want to invite Mrs. Gird to the wedding or whatever it was, Zellie thought unkindly. It was hard to imagine Mrs. Gird having a good time. It was hard to imagine her *smiling* for more than a few seconds.

"I had better go now," Zellie said, suddenly aware that now she *was* dawdling for no good reason.

"I thank you for the help," Miss O'Brien told her. "I do hope you will come join the girls at their class tonight. I think you would be most interested in their discussions."

Zellie nodded, wishing she could come but knowing that she would almost certainly not be allowed to attend. There would be a mountain of dishes to wash and the whole kitchen to clean again.

Zellie walked as fast as she could on the way back. She was breathing hard by the time she stepped up onto the back porch. She set the bag down in the trampled snow to open the door, then picked it up again and lugged it inside.

"Where have you been?" Mrs. Gird demanded,

turning from the hearth to glare at Zellie. "Bring them here, let's get them washed."

Zellie let out a long breath, pulling off her coat in one swift motion. She hung it on the nail by the door, then picked up the bag and walked to the drainboard.

"We need more water," Mrs. Gird said.

Zellie nodded without speaking. Mrs. Gird didn't seem to care if she spoke or not. So she didn't bother. Instead, she took the bucket from its hook and went outside. When she came back in, she poured the fresh water into the stout barrel beside the drainboard, then went to fetch more.

"That's enough," Mrs. Gird said after the sixth bucket. Zellie sighed and hung it back up, her arms aching. The potatoes had been heavy. A full oak bucket was even heavier. At least the well wasn't too far from the house, and it was shallow. With the rivers and the canals, water was everywhere in Lowell.

"Get the potatoes washed as quick as you can," Mrs. Gird said tersely, interrupting Zellie's thoughts. She nodded and lifted the potato sack onto the drainboard. Then, careful to wipe off as much of the soil as she could, she dropped the potatoes one by one into the basin of cold water.

"Here." Mrs. Gird handed her a stiff pig-bristle brush. Zellie took it and set to work, trying to hurry. If the potatoes weren't done by suppertime, Mrs. Gird would surely blame her for whatever trouble it caused.

As she worked, Zellie tried to figure out what to do with Lydia's paper. While all the girls were in the room, eating, there would be no chance to give it to her and explain what had happened. And after supper, when the girls were leaving to go to Miss O'Brien's store . . . it would be even harder. Maybe she could find a way to slip it into Lydia's writing box. Of course she'd still have to explain to Lydia how the paper ended up in the box, but at least it would be in a safe place—and she'd be rid of it.

"They're clean," Zellie announced when she finished.

Mrs. Gird was laying the plated-ware on the tables. "Get them cut up, then."

"To roast or boil?" Zellie asking, hoping they were going to roast them—that meant bigger pieces.

"Cut them small and we'll boil them in the soup," Mrs. Gird said. "They'll be expecting roast tonight, but they may as well get used to soup—if they don't want their wages cut so my fees can be raised. . . ."

Zellie turned, hoping Mrs. Gird would go on, but she didn't. "Why would their wages get cut?" Zellie asked.

Mrs. Gird scowled. "Just get the potatoes in the pot."

Zellie sighed and laid out the cutting board and got a knife. It was razor sharp and she worked carefully, keeping her mind on what she was doing. Only when the last of the potatoes had been cut into small chunks did she glance up. "Shall I put them in the pot now?"

"Yes." Mrs. Gird looked out the window and Zellie followed her glance. It was getting dusky but the girls wouldn't be home for quite a while. They didn't stop work until seven o'clock. The potatoes would have plenty of time to boil down and thicken the soup. Zellie carried the basin to the hearth and began to scoop the potatoes into the iron cauldron.

"Set out water cups and pitchers, then clean off the drainboard and stoke the fire," Mrs. Gird said, walking toward the door. "Then light the lamps when you are finished in here," Mrs. Gird called back over her shoulder as she left the kitchen.

"Yes, Ma'am," Zellie answered. She took a deep breath. It was time to decide. Lamp lighting would give her an excuse to go upstairs. If she was going to put the paper in Lydia's writing box, this would probably be her only chance.

"Should I?" she asked herself aloud. Then she shook her head, uncertain. It might cause more trouble, not less. Zellie sighed and forced herself to stop thinking and start working.

Once she was finished with the potatoes, she

filled pitchers and glasses with water and set them on the tables. Finally, she took a candleholder from the shelf above the drainboard and lit the wick before she started down the dark hall. Halfway to the storeroom, she shivered. Anywhere away from the hearth, the house was cold.

The two high windows in the storeroom were darkening fast as Zellie lined up the lamps. She lit one and adjusted the two wicks and set the candleholder on the shelf by the door. Sighing a little, her feet icy cold in her still-damp stockings, she picked up the lamp and went back into the long hallway.

Mrs. Gird was not one to waste expensive lamp oil or candles, Zellie thought as she climbed the stairs. After all, she had to pay for them! She probably liked the nights when most of the girls trouped off to classes and lectures. It would save her money. If they were all home, the girls would be asking for candles to write letters or read their lending-library books or do needlework.

At ten o'clock, of course, Mrs. Gird counted the girls and then all upstairs lights would be put out. Then Mrs. Gird got her keys and locked the back door until morning. No one used the front door. Mrs. Gird kept it locked all the time.

Climbing the stairs to the first floor, Zellie longed for a book to read. She wished she dared ask to borrow one. But she knew she couldn't. Not in Mrs. Gird's house.

She set the lamp on its little round side table, then went back to light the second-floor lamp, then the third floor's.

Zellie hurried back up the stairs and set the last one down very gently, noticing a sheen on the tabletop. She ran her hand over the surface. It was just the beeswax that had been rubbed into the wood—not spilled oil. Zellie exhaled, glad she wouldn't have to clean up a mess. Even a little spilled oil was dangerous.

Grandmamma had hated these new astral lamps, Zellie thought as she stared at the bright light, putting off making her decision about the paper for another moment. They were too bright for a person's eyes, Grandmamma had always said. Candlelight was best. Zellie smiled. Homemade candles had been good enough for Grandmamma's mother and they had been good enough for her.

"Fire is danger enough," Grandmamma had said a hundred times. "Why add lamp oil to it?"

Zellie could hear her Grandmother's voice so perfectly in her mind that it made her smile again. "No one will start a fire here, Grandmamma," she said aloud. "These are all farm girls. There's not a witless, prissy rich girl in the whole house—none of that kind works in a factory."

Zellie sighed, missing her grandmother so much that it hurt. Then she turned to stare at the door to Lydia's room. She knew she had to decide. Time was running out.

Zellie made a quick list in her mind.

1. She could put the paper in Lydia's writing box, then explain to Lydia later how she had found it. If she told the truth, it might be all right.
2. But if she returned it this way, and told Lydia, how could she explain knowing about the writing box?
3. If she put the paper in the writing box and never explained anything, what would Lydia do? Maybe she would assume that one of her friends had done it—even if they denied it. And even if she suspected that Zellie had, why would she mind? So long as no trouble came from it, what reason would she have to be upset?

Zellie sighed. More than anything, she wanted to get rid of the paper, to stop worrying about it. Why should it be this complicated? She wasn't stealing anything. She was *returning* something. She could figure out whether to explain to Lydia later.

On impulse, Zellie lifted the lamp and went into Lydia's room. Keeping her back to the window, she set the lantern among the knickknacks on the dresser. Then she leaned across the neatly made bed.

Nervous, her breath coming fast because she felt so *wrong* doing something so sneaky, Zellie felt her way along the smooth, cool plaster, then started back, bending lower to find the box with her outstretched fingers.

But it wasn't there.

Lydia must have moved it at noontime.

Zellie frowned, trying to remember if Lydia had left the kitchen. Then she straightened up, listening for Mrs. Gird's heavy steps on the stairs. The last thing she needed was to get caught doing something as impossible to explain as this.

Feeling close to tears, Zellie carried the astral lamp back out and set it where it was meant to go. She started toward the head of the stairs, glancing nervously at the landing window. Outside the dusk was deepening into night.

Zellie blinked, making herself look a moment longer, her heart speeding up. The view out the window didn't scare her quite as much now. It was getting so dark that she couldn't really see the wide strip of grassy weeds or the wide river beyond the red brick buildings of the mill. She couldn't see the ground at all.

Forcing herself to take another step toward the window, she tried to still her heart, to slow her ragged breathing. What in the world would she do if Mrs. Gird told her to wash the window glass? She shuddered. She would no more be able to stand that close to the window in the daytime and look out than the man in the moon could come down to swim in the Merrimack River.

A sudden flash of white caught Zellie's eye and she stared. A girl? Running toward the back door?

Zellie caught her breath. Had someone seen her rummaging through Lydia's room from the dark yard below? She ran toward the stairs.

CHAPTER NINE

Zellie bolted down the stairs. She knew that that running only made her look like she was truly guilty of something, but she couldn't slow her pace until she was halfway up the hall, passing the storeroom.

Only then did she begin to hear her own thoughts spinning in frantic circles. Maybe she should hide the paper somewhere . . . right now. What if Lydia burst in the back door, accusing her of going through her belongings? She hadn't taken the paper from Lydia's room, but that was certainly what Mrs. Gird would think. And that was the way it would look if someone found the paper tucked inside her bodice. But where would it be safe?

"In the bottom of the rag bin," she said aloud, and pushed open the storeroom door.

It was dark inside, but the bin was by the wall and she felt her way toward it. Reaching down, she slid the paper beneath the knee-high pile of cleaning cloths.

Then coming out through the door silently, she looked both ways before she walked away quickly, all the way down the hall to the kitchen and hurried through the doorway.

"Finished?" Mrs. Gird asked. She was sitting on a stool by the hearth, stirring the soup. Zellie saw the two Dutch ovens in the ashes.

"Stoke the fire," Mrs. Gird called. "Then fill the wood box. Use the woodpile stacked against the front wall." She jerked her chin in that direction.

Zellie pulled in a quick breath. "Yes, Ma'am," she answered, hoping she didn't sound as shaky as she felt. She carefully placed two slim logs on the back of the fire, away from the Dutch ovens. The last thing she wanted to do was to burn the corn bread. She felt the hair on her forearms sizzle as she leaned into the wide hearth.

Then she stepped back and started for the back door. She pulled on her coat and went out. It was nearly dark. She walked fast, trying to delay the snow from soaking into her stockings.

"*Pssst!*"

The sound made Zellie jump backward and she whirled in a circle, trying to spot whoever was there.

"Zellie!" It was a whisper.

"Who's there?" she whispered back.

"It's Lydia."

Zellie caught her breath. Had Lydia been looking

through the lighted window? Had Lydia seen her lean-ing over the bed?

"Zellie! Will you help me?" Lydia hissed.

Zellie stared into the gathering darkness. Maybe Lydia hadn't seen her? She began to hope. "What's wrong?"

"I left a paper in the storeroom and . . . it's . . . something I need," she said carefully.

Zellie hesitated, wondering what to say.

"Look, Zellie," Lydia burst out, "Plumy just told me that Mrs. Gird said she was going to do the linen laundry today. Did she?"

Zellie was silent, her heart thudding.

"It's always on Mondays," Lydia said. Her voice sounded tight, desperate.

"We did it today," Zellie told her.

Lydia made a sound of dismay and stepped for-ward. She was wearing a white dress. Zellie felt sure it *had* been her, running along the far side of the house. But if she had happened to look through the lighted window, she showed no sign of it. She looked scared, not angry.

Lydia wiped a hand across her mouth and shifted her weight from one foot to the other. "Zellie? Did Mrs. Gird find it?"

Zellie shook her head. "I did. And I didn't show it to her."

Lydia cried out softly. "Oh, Zellie. I was hoping

you had found it and would have the sense to keep it to yourself! Where is it?"

"It's inside the house," she told Lydia. "It's hidden."

Lydia leaned toward her. "Hidden?"

Zellie nodded. "I put it at the bottom of the rag bin in the storeroom." She hesitated, then decided to tell the whole truth. "I thought about putting it in your room, but I—"

"I am just so grateful," Lydia interrupted her. Then she let out a long breath. "Thank you so much. I owe you a favor, Zellie," she said.

Zellie shook her head, but Lydia went right on. "I'll get it this evening, then. I'll explain all this soon, I promise."

And then, without saying another word, she whirled around and ran back across the dark yard. Zellie could hear her footsteps receding as she sprinted back toward the mill, running as fast as her skirt would let her.

"How did she slip out of the weaving room to come here?" Zellie asked the empty night sky. "She must have been really worried to do that." And she began to wonder what the papers were really about. It had to be something a lot more important than a guest list.

The stars were covered with clouds still, but Zellie imagined that she could see them. Grandmamma had loved the stars.

"What is taking you so long?" Mrs. Gird's voice was edged with irritation.

"It's dark," Zellie said in a wavering voice.

"There's nothing to be afraid of," Mrs. Gird said, misunderstanding why Zellie sounded upset. Then she laughed, a sharp, grating sound. "Afraid of the dark at your age?"

"I'm hurrying," Zellie called.

"See that you do!" Mrs. Gird answered. "At this rate I'll have to lock you out at ten!"

Zellie heard the sound of Mrs. Gird jingling her keys for emphasis, then the sound of the back door closing. Mrs. Gird wouldn't leave it ajar even for a few minutes because the kitchen's heat would flow out instead of down the hall and up the stairs.

Zellie took a deep breath and stared for another moment in the direction of the mill. What was Lydia planning? It wasn't a wedding or a party, Zellie was almost sure, now.

Zellie stacked her arms high with the small logs, then started back for the door. She was halfway there when she heard it open.

"Zellie!" Mrs. Gird shouted again.

"Coming!" she called back, careful to keep her voice even.

As she walked through the door, Zellie saw Mrs. Gird walking toward the sideboard. A pile of apples lay on it and a knife. Mrs. Gird didn't even glance up, so

Zellie dropped the load of wood into the firebox and hurried back outside.

It took six trips to the woodpile to fill the box beside the hearth, and Zellie's fingers and nose were ice cold by the time she finished. Her feet were wet again.

"Have you overheard anything among the girls?" Mrs. Gird asked as she hung her coat back on the nail.

Zellie was caught off guard and didn't know what to say. "No," she said finally, telling the truth, but barely. Her voice sounded tight and she knew that Mrs. Gird had heard the odd tone when she frowned.

"You had better not be keeping their secrets, Zellie," she warned. "Remember who you work for."

"I don't know anything," Zellie began.

"Nonsense," Mrs. Gird interrupted. "You must have heard something by now. They don't hush when you come to the table with milk or extra corn bread like they do when I pass by."

Zellie nodded. That was probably true. She overheard a lot of conversations in the kitchen but most of them weren't interesting and she paid little attention.

Zellie took a deep breath. "They talk about the lectures they are going to in the evenings and letters home and beaus and missing their brothers and sisters. And they talk about the lending library and each other's hairstyles and—"

American Diaries

"I know all that," Mrs. Gird interrupted her. "But they also talk about something they shouldn't be talking about. Mr. Thissel, the mill agent, came by today. He says there are rumors of a turn-out."

Zellie looked at her blankly. What was a turn-out?

"Stir the coals around the Dutch ovens," Mrs. Gird said sharply, "and make sure you sweep the hearth clean so you don't track ashes everywhere."

"I'll stir the soup," Zellie said, trying to sound pleasant. "It smells very good."

Mrs. Gird shook her head. "If boarding fees don't go up, I can't afford to feed them anything but soup. *Their* precious wages! With cloth prices so far down, there's no other solution."

Zellie watched as Mrs. Gird turned on her heel and walked away. The grocer had said something about the boardinghouse fees, too. Zellie tried to remember his exact words, and she couldn't.

"Mrs. Gird is impossible to please," Zellie whispered to herself as she worked the fire rake back and forth, stirring the coals around the Dutch ovens to keep them hot enough to bake the corn bread all the way through. She accidentally pushed ashes up onto the hearth and bent low to grab the horsehair broom and swept them back in.

"And the truth is, I don't much like her," she whispered as she put the little broom back on its hook and stirred the soup slowly.

Zellie looked around the room. The tables were laid out, the food was nearly ready. And at that instant, she heard voices outside. The girls were coming.

Zellie took a deep breath. She would try hard to hear something about the turn-out, whatever *that* was. Maybe that would make Mrs. Gird happy enough to keep her working. At least now she had some idea what she was supposed to be listening for.

"I have to hear enough to keep this position," she told herself. "At least long enough to buy a pair of shoes."

CHAPTER TEN

The girls poured into the room. They were rosy cheeked and noisy, then quieted as they got their coats off and hung them over the backs of their chairs. They lined up in an orderly way and nearly every one of them politely thanked Zellie for giving her a bowl of the soup.

"Miss O'Brien asked me to tell you to please come tonight," Lydia said when her turn came.

"She did?" Zellie asked, surprised.

Lydia nodded. "She said both the discussion and the class would interest you, she was sure."

"Plumy says she will help you clean up after supper so you can. I would help, too, but I have to do . . . something else," she said, still smiling.

She looked excited, Zellie thought, like someone expecting a surprise. Then Lydia walked away and Plumy stepped up. "I *will* help. Mrs. Gird won't mind if you go, will she?"

Zellie shrugged. "She won't let me go. But I will ask her."

All through supper, Zellie tried to listen for anyone talking about a turn-out. She heard nothing but the same kind of chatting she had heard all along.

The girls were homesick and they talked about their families and their men friends and their clothes and the lectures they had heard recently. They talked about books and poems.

One girl sitting across from Plumy went on and on about her little dog. She had left it with her mother and it sounded like she missed it more than the rest of her family.

Mrs. Gird walked up and down between the tables, smiling at the girls. A smile looked unnatural on her face, Zellie thought.

"More corn bread over here," she called to Zellie, pointing at a table with an empty bread plate. Not only did the smile look odd, even her voice sounded different. She was pretending to be nice, Zellie realized. Why?

Once the girls were finished eating and on their way up the stairs to their rooms, Lydia and Plumy walked slowly past the hearth where Zellie stood, waiting to clear off the tables.

"I asked Mrs. Gird if you could come with us," Lydia said. "She said it was all right, once the work was done."

"She did?" Zellie asked, astonished.

Lydia nodded.

"I'll help and then we can be ready when Lydia is," Plumy said. Zellie stared at her. She looked like a different person from the homesick, pale girl who had gotten off the stage.

"Zellie?"

Zellie glanced at Mrs. Gird. As she came across the room, she was still smiling at any of the girls who happened to glance at her.

"Plumy," Mrs. Gird said pleasantly as she got close. "You can start clearing while Zellie gets the dishwater ready."

Plumy nodded and hurried to the back of the room, starting with the tables farthest from the drainboard.

"Did you overhear anything at supper?" Miss Gird asked when Plumy was busy at the far end of the room. Her voice was low and she stood close—too close. She smelled sour and sweaty.

Zellie shook her head uneasily. "Nothing besides what I told you." She was tempted to add that she had no idea what a turn-out was, but she didn't. She would find out. She would ask Lydia.

"Well this improvement class should be a good place to find out what they are up to," Mrs. Gird said. "And you can make up the time tomorrow night," she added, still smiling.

"Yes, Ma'am," Zellie said unhappily. She should have known that Mrs. Gird wouldn't really be generous.

Making up the time would mean working fifteen or sixteen hours the next day instead of her usual thirteen or fourteen. "Maybe I should just stay here," she said aloud.

Mrs. Gird frowned. "No. You have to go."

Zellie sighed and asked, even though she knew the answer. "Why?"

"Because even if they don't say anything important at their little class, they will be talking all the way to the millinery, and again when they walk home. And they will not be nearly as careful as they are here."

Zellie sighed, and decided to tell the truth after all. "Mrs. Gird," she said quietly. "I don't even know what a turn-out is."

Mrs. Gird scowled, then she shook her head. "It means they walk off. They leave their looms."

Zellie tried to make sense out of what Mrs. Gird was saying. "They walk off?"

Mrs. Gird nodded.

"Where do they go?" Zellie asked. "If they just leave, won't they lose their jobs?"

"Of course!" Mrs. Gird exploded. Then she dropped her voice to a whisper. "But their wages are about to get cut. They think if they turn out, the mill owners won't do it." She leaned closer. "Lydia likes you, and I think she's one of the organizers."

Zellie felt her heart thud harder. The papers she'd seen. The lists of names . . . Lydia might be making lists of girls who had agreed to walk out of the mill. What had the paper in Lydia's writing box said? Something about the girls who would "come with us"?

"But won't they just get into trouble?" she asked Mrs. Gird again. She couldn't imagine doing anything so foolish as losing her position on purpose.

Mrs. Gird waved a hand to silence her. "You just listen for all you're worth and tell me everything you hear. If I can stop the ones from this house from going, the mill agent will be grateful," she said. "Help me do that and you can stay here all winter. Maybe longer. I give you my word on it."

Zellie let out a breath as Mrs. Gird walked away quickly, pretending to be happy again. She smiled at Plumy and even carried one load of dirty bowls to the sideboard before she went out of the kitchen.

Once she was gone, Zellie worked hard. With Plumy helping, the whole kitchen was clean in such a short time that Zellie found herself humming. Maybe everything would be all right after all. If the girls talked about the usual things, there would be nothing to tell Mrs. Gird. Zellie smiled. But if they did, she could tell Mrs. Gird just enough to keep her position.

The next day would be tiring, but maybe it would be worth it. She would get out of the stuffy house and get to see Miss O'Brien again. "Almost finished?" Lydia asked, walking into the kitchen. Zellie saw a flash of cream-colored paper in the girl's hand as she slipped it inside her own dress bodice.

"Thanks again, Zellie," she whispered, leaning close. Then she stepped back and lifted her chin. "Have you eaten?"

Zellie shook her head, glancing around to be sure no one else had seen Lydia holding the paper. Then she walked over to the drainboard and reached down into the cracker box.

"Mrs. Gird has you keep your dishes down there?" Lydia asked.

Zellie glanced at her, trying to read her expression. "Yes."

Lydia bit at her lip. "Because you are . . ."

"Negro," Zellie finished for her. "Yes."

"Were your parents slaves?" Lydia asked.

"Lydia!" Plumy chided, walking closer.

Zellie ladled soup into her bowl, turning her back on Lydia, hoping she would find something else to talk about. There were so many abolitionists in Massachusetts—and she was grateful. But Grandmamma had said it more than once: Some white people were just too curious about things they couldn't ever understand anyway.

"No," Zellie said evenly and clearly. "All the way back to my great-grandmother we have been born free."

Lydia pressed her lips together, but then she smiled.

Zellie sat at a table close to the hearth. Plumy brought her corn bread and she smiled her thanks, then concentrated on eating. She was hungry and she ate fast.

"Are you ready to go?" Lydia asked Plumy.

"I am," Plumy told her.

Zellie glanced up and saw Lydia smiling at Plumy. "Thank you so much for helping Zellie so she could come tonight."

Plumy smiled. "I enjoy working, really. And I didn't do anything at the mill today except watch, so I don't mind."

"I thank you too, Plumy," Zellie said.

Plumy gestured dismissively. "I didn't mind a bit. Honestly." Then she sighed. "My first day at Lowell hasn't been so bad thanks to you both. I don't think I will die of homesickness, after all." She had her head tipped back and spoke, looking upward, as though giving thanks that her first day in Lowell had not been as bad as she had feared.

Lydia laughed. "I told you so."

Plumy nodded. "You did. And you were right. I'll still miss my family terribly, but—"

"We all do," Lydia interrupted. She interrupted a lot, Zellie realized, but her smile was so nice and she was so pretty, people didn't mind.

"Where is your family, Zellie?" Lydia asked. "Here in Lowell?"

Zellie shook her head, frowning. She didn't want to answer so many questions. "I don't have family now," she said, truthfully, then closed her mouth firmly, hoping that Lydia would take the hint.

But Lydia only looked at her intently. "No one?"

Zellie shook her head, wishing she hadn't said anything. She didn't want to try to explain her Auntie Persis or anything else to this brash girl.

Lydia met her eyes. "Are your parents? . . ."

Zellie glared at her. "My father was killed before I was born. My mother died of a fever when I was six. Is there anything else you need to know?"

Lydia frowned and Zellie felt her heart thudding inside her chest. That had been just plain stupid. What was wrong with her, bursting out rudely at a white girl like that? If Mrs. Gird had heard her, she might be on her way out the door at this very instant.

"I'm very sorry," she made herself say.

Lydia shook her head. "*I'm* sorry, Zellie. I had no right to push at you like that."

"I'll say," Plumy agreed.

Lydia blushed. "I have nine brothers and two sisters," she said. She shook her head. "And more cousins than I can count. I just can't imagine . . ." she trailed off, her eyes full of sympathy and kindness.

"That's why my family sent me to Lowell," Plumy said, moving close to the hearth. "There are too many at home, and my poor brother can't work at all after his accident last month. I can send money home, I hope, and at least they don't have to feed me. I think all my sisters will follow."

Zellie nodded, glad that they had begun to talk about themselves instead of about her.

"My sister came here two years past," Lydia was saying. "They got paid the same as we do now—and they only had one loom to watch."

Plumy tilted her head. "But you do two looms now."

Lydia nodded. "I do. And there's talk of them going to four. Everyone does more work now than they did before. More work for the same pay."

"I'm ready when you are," a dark-haired girl said, coming into the kitchen from the long hall.

Lydia looked up. "And the others?"

The girl nodded, walking toward them so they could hear her as she lowered her voice. "I think most of the others are coming—but they want to go in small groups to attract less attention in town."

Lydia's eyes narrowed. "They will need to gather their courage by tomorrow and stop caring what anyone thinks!"

The dark-haired girl glanced at Zellie and her meaning was clear. She wasn't sure Lydia should be talking so freely.

"Zellie is going with us. Miss O'Brien asked for her company." The girl's eyebrows went up and Lydia nodded. "Abigale," she said evenly. "Have you met Zellie properly?"

Abigale shook her head and Lydia gave a graceful introduction. After they had exchanged polite murmurs, Zellie glanced at Lydia.

"Shall we go?" Lydia asked. Plumy and Abigale nodded. Lydia met Zellie's eyes again. "Are you ready?"

Zellie smiled. She picked up her dishes and walked to the drainboard to wash them out. As she pulled on her ragged coat, she glanced at Lydia's nice one. Abigale's was smooth, tightly woven wool, too, the color of wheat. Only Plumy had a hand-me-down that looked like it had been worn for years.

As they set off, Zellie dropped back to walk beside Plumy, her thoughts spinning in circles. These girls seemed so lucky to her. They had good work and their wages were enough that they bought nice clothes for themselves and went to lectures and classes in the evenings—and *still* were able to send money home to their families. . . .

And they *had* families. Zellie sighed and Plumy glanced at her, but didn't say anything.

Zellie was grateful.

CHAPTER ELEVEN

Lydia and Abigale were laughing and talking, their heads close together as they crossed the canal bridge and started down Central Street. It was cold. Zellie hunched her shoulders and tried to ignore the icy intrusion of snow into her shoes.

The shop was warm, at least. As they made their way inside, Zellie pulled in a long breath of warm air. There were already voices in the big back room. She followed Lydia and Abigale past the hats and dress forms and bolts of fabric in the front of the shop.

"There you are!" Miss O'Brien said when she saw them. She smiled at Lydia and Abigale and motioned for them to come in. Then when she saw Zellie, Miss O'Brien's smiled widened. "I have something to tell you," she said, drawing her aside.

Zellie glanced back to make sure that Plumy was catching up with Lydia and Abigale. A circle of girls stood on the far side of the room, talking quietly.

"I just wanted to tell you that Mrs. Thissel loved

the hat. She looked at the stitch work and told me she'd never seen a finer job."

Zellie smiled. "Almost all of that stitch work was yours."

"I know," Miss O'Brien said. "And I *am* a genius with a needle. So perhaps you should believe it when I say you might have a future in millinery work if you want it."

Zellie blinked. Miss O'Brien would never mean to be cruel, she was sure. And it had been kind of her to say Grandmamma's headache cure would pay for this class. But one class hardly meant a future at anything. As much as she would love to imagine herself as a milliner, working in her own little shop one day, she knew better. She would not have money to pay for classes, much less a real apprenticeship.

"Pay attention," she murmured to herself beneath the noise of the conversations all around her. "Remember everything you can for Mrs. Gird."

Miss O'Brien frowned and touched Zellie's arm as she turned abruptly to face the doorway. "Oh, my," she said. She nodded toward three girls following an older woman into the room. Zellie stared at them. They all looked deadly serious, their faces set and their eyes fierce.

"These four always want a turn-out," Miss O'Brien whispered as the little group came in and found seats along the walls. "They are known as troublemakers even among those of us who share their beliefs. I was hoping they might not come."

Zellie nodded, though she didn't really understand.

"Most of us want to be reasonable," Miss O'Brien added. "These things take time."

"Hello!" a cheerful voice called from the doorway. Zellie looked back at a line of familiar faces as the girls from Mrs. Gird's boardinghouse began arriving. She recognized most of them—and they nodded politely at her, though some of them looked surprised to see her.

They were all nicely dressed and Zellie looked down at her coat again. She fiddled with the worn sleeve until she noticed Miss O'Brien watching her. Then she took the coat off and laid it over her arm. Her dress wasn't much better, she knew; it was actually worse, smudged with potato dirt and splatters from her other chores.

"Let's get started," Lydia was saying.

Zellie turned to face her, grateful. It did no good to think about her worn-out clothes. There was nothing she could do about them until Mrs. Gird paid her and she could begin to save her pennies. As Zellie watched, the girls sat down, many of them pairing up to share a single chair. The room was *crowded*.

"We have found a lecturer for next month," Lydia said. "He's a scientific abolitionist from Boston and a fine speechifier." She smiled around the room. "We will owe a penny apiece if we can get thirty to come. Fewer and we will owe more," she added. "So tell your friends."

"Where?" someone asked from the far side of the room.

"Probably the Baptist church," Lydia answered. "But we aren't sure yet. Amanda? Do you know about the reading groups?"

A dark-haired girl stood up and blushed as she faced the others. "We continue to read and discuss Mary Wollstonecraft's *A Vindication of the Rights of Woman,* here in the shop, every Thursday evening. We are picking up a few more every week. Most of them are here so I won't bother to tell what it's about."

There was a round of quiet laughter. Miss O'Brien leaned close to Zellie's ear. "The book is about women being full human beings. I mean human first, women second. Human first, then all the rest comes after—gender, age," she met Zellie's eyes, then leaned closer. "It makes sense, I think. Small or tall, German or Greek or African or English or American, fat or thin, Christian or Hindi, and so on. But we are all human first." She straightened up, leaving a faint scent of lavender in the air beside Zellie's face.

The talking went on and Zellie listened, but it

was hard to keep from thinking at the same time. These girls were saying things she had never heard anywhere before in her whole life.

"The bank is going to let us handle our own accounts soon," the older, fierce-looking woman stated flatly. "They will soon let us withdraw our own money—with or without a male relative to sign the papers."

A fluttering of excitement passed through the crowd.

"Who told you this?" Miss O'Brien asked politely.

"A banker!" the woman answered, smiling. "It's true this time."

Miss O'Brien nodded. "Will it only be the mill girls, or can any woman manage her own account?"

The woman frowned. "I would hope anyone. But part of their reason for allowing it is that the mill companies want some of the wages they pay out to stay in Lowell—not all be sent home with a friend or neighbor to make some other community richer."

"We are hoping that Negro people will be included soon," the woman said, nodding politely at Zellie. "And children who are employed. There is no reason why a lot of nonsense can't be cleared away before long."

The girls began to talk all at once, and Zellie could only hear segments and snatches of conversations around her. They were talking about slavery and the damage alcohol did to people and the sad lives of poor elderly people and what they would do if they could vote as men did.

"Do you read and write?" Miss O'Brien asked, leaning close again.

Zellie nodded. "I've had nearly five years of school."

Miss O'Brien smiled and her eyes twinkled. "Perfect," she said. And then she stood up straight again and began talking to the mill girl on her right. Zellie blinked, puzzled, then refocused on the girls' conversations. Did Mrs. Gird want to know all of this, too, all this talk about banking their own wages and ending slavery and . . . voting? Zellie swallowed and looked around the room. Probably not. She had said she just wanted to stop the turn-out from her own house.

Zellie tried to find someone in the crowd around her talking about walking off from work, but no one was. She stared at one girl, then another and knew no one would notice. They were all so serious, their faces intent as they spoke to one another.

Then the girl Zellie was watching glanced up. Zellie noticed others doing the same.

"Order, please," Lydia was saying, a little more loudly each time.

The conversations around Zellie thinned, until only a few voices were heard, their words rushed as they tried to finish what they'd begun. Then there were only a few whispers.

"We have decided on tomorrow," Lydia said—and suddenly there was silence.

"So we really mean it this time?" a girl near the door asked. Her face was tense. "I thought we might write up a stronger petition and—"

"It doesn't do any good and you know it," Lydia said. "The only way the companies are going to listen to us is if we stop the mills."

"But cloth prices are still falling," someone said.

A chorus of voices stopped her from saying anything more.

"If the prices have dropped, does that mean we work less hard to make the cloth?" Lydia countered when the girls had quieted. "Most of us work more than eighty hours a week! If we said we were going to cut our hours and expected our pay to stay the same, what would they tell us?"

"If we walk out, they won't let us come back," another girl said. She looked terrified. "I know many of you don't have to have the wages. But some of us are supporting our parents and—"

"We've all agreed to help any girl who hasn't got the fare to get back home," Lydia said. "We've signed petitions to include that and we'll pass them around at the turn-out."

"Fare home is one thing," the girl answered in a

strained voice. "But I mean another thing entirely. My parents can't live without what I send them."

"We understand your position, Janie," Lydia said. Then she hesitated. "And if you don't walk out, there's not a soul in this room who will think any less of you for it." Lydia paused a second time. "But we can't let it stop the rest us, can we?"

Zellie thought Janie might start crying, but she didn't. Instead she lifted her head. "I wish you success; I simply cannot join you."

There were soft murmurs around the room. Zellie saw one or two of the other girls take deep breaths as though they were about to speak, but then they only sighed.

"Anyone who cannot join us," Lydia said, "will be understood and forgiven. We ask only that you don't betray us beforehand. Our boardinghouse keeper would stop us if she could."

"She'd lock us in our rooms if it made Mr. Thissel think better of her," a girl from Mrs. Gird's house said. The others laughed quietly, nodding.

Lydia glanced around the room, then her eyes rested on Zellie's for a long moment. Zellie swallowed hard. Did Lydia know that Mrs. Gird expected her to do exactly that . . . betray these girls?

Zellie looked down at her feet.

"A ten-hour working day is our goal," Lydia said,

"But for now our purpose is to keep them from lowering our wages."

"I think the boardinghouse keepers are helping to push this along," Abigale said, her face flushing when all turned to look at her. "If the companies lower our wages, they can pay a little more to the boardinghouse women."

Zellie felt a cold chill on the back of her neck. Was that it? Mrs. Gird wants to stop the turn-out so she would make more money. She had said almost as much herself.

Zellie swallowed hard. The mill girls cared desperately about their positions and their wages—but she cared just as much about her own.

The little room was so crowded that the air began to feel thick—too thick—filled with the scents of lavender and damp wool. But the girls kept on, talking about women in England fighting much worse factory conditions, about being afraid to walk out, about being determined to do it anyway. Zellie watched their faces go from brave to scared, then back again.

By the time the meeting was over—without a single moment spent on needlework of any kind—Zellie was desperate to get outside into the fresh air.

"Take care, Zellie," Miss O'Brien said as they were leaving. "Come visit when you can. If Bertha will let you come to real classes, consider the Wollstonecraft book discussions. She wrote that book forty-two years ago and people have been talking about it since. What an accomplishment!"

Zellie murmured a polite answer, knowing that Mrs. Gird would never let her attend another class or meeting of any kind unless she told her something she wanted to hear.

"There are lectures once or twice a week on every topic. And classes. And we'll have a meeting here next week. There are so many wrongs to right in this world."

"Yes, Ma'am," Zellie answered, not knowing what else to say. She felt a prickling on the back of her neck. It was exciting, thinking about all the ways the world should be different. "Grandmamma always said every child should go to school," she said, without knowing she was going to say it.

"I think your grandmother and I would have been friends," Miss O'Brien said. "I told you about the Lewis family," she added. "Three of their daughters are teachers. Maybe you should think about that instead of millinery. Or learn both."

Zellie fumbled at getting her coat back on and said a mumbled goodnight to Miss O'Brien. All this talk made her feel strange and restless. She edged toward the door and went outside to wait.

Lydia stayed until nearly everyone else had gone.

Zellie and Plumy stood shivering just outside while she and Abigale spoke in low voices to Miss O'Brien.

Then finally it was time to walk home. All the way back to the boardinghouse, Zellie hurried along, staying a little apart from the others, still taking in big gulps of the fresh air. The others were talking. Lydia was explaining to Plumy how the overseers would be insulted—all of them were fatherly men who thought of the mill girls as ladylike and refined.

"They are going think us perfect Amazons," she said sadly, "unfeminine monsters." They reached the porch and went up the steps. Then she fell silent.

Mrs. Gird was in the kitchen when they came in, fiddling with the fire rake. She turned from the hearth and looked at the girls, her false smile in place. "You're the last ones home. Was it a good needlework class?" she asked.

Lydia smiled and didn't answer beyond a vague nod. Plumy murmured something about being very tired. At the hall door, Lydia turned. "Thank you for coming with us, Zellie," she said. "Isn't it interesting what we can all teach each other?"

Zellie nodded, feeling Mrs. Gird's eyes on her as she did it. Then the girls were gone.

"Well?" Mrs. Gird demanded.

Zellie took a long breath. She meant to tell Mrs. Gird about what she had heard. She intended to keep her position. But somehow she felt her grandmother standing close and she lifted her head and said, "It was very interesting. Miss O'Brien says I might be a seamstress one day. Or a teacher."

Then she walked to the folded blankets beside the hearth and began to lay out her makeshift bed. Mrs. Gird made an angry sound, muttered something, then walked stiffly out of the kitchen.

CHAPTER TWELVE

The next morning, Zellie could feel the tension in the air and she knew that Mrs. Gird could too. Most of the girls were quiet, and the few that were talking seemed to talk too loudly.

Once they had gone out the back door and were walking in the gray-dawn light toward the mill, Mrs. Gird went back to her room.

Grateful that Mrs. Gird hadn't questioned her further, Zellie set about setting the house to rights, making beds and straightening the parlor.

Her thoughts kept straying to the big, brick mill buildings. Were the girls really going to do it? Would enough of them have the courage for a turn-out? Her mind uneasy, Zellie headed for the kitchen to check the hearth fire. She was bent over the wood box when she heard footsteps.

"I am going to walk to town," Mrs. Gird said from the hallway door.

Zellie jumped, startled.

Mrs. Gird came to stand by the hearth, warming her hands a moment. "When you are through with the beds, clean the washrooms, then fill the water barrel and the wood box."

Then she turned on her heel and walked out. She slammed the back door behind herself. Zellie stood still, both relieved and anxious. Why would Mrs. Gird decide to go to town this morning? "If there was an errand, she'd send me," Zellie said aloud.

Zellie shook her head. There was absolutely no use in trying to figure out why Mrs. Gird would do anything. Puzzled and feeling uneasy, she started her work.

She was finishing the third-floor washroom when she heard the back door slam.

"Zellie?!"

It was Lydia's voice. "Zellie, are you here?" Footsteps were pounding up the hallway and Zellie crossed the landing, avoiding the view of the dizzying drop outside the window. "Up here!"

Lydia came running up the stairs, holding her skirt above her knees to take the steps two at a time, her face flushed. "Did you tell her?" she demanded.

Zellie shook her head. "No. But I think she knew. She left here about—"

"I know," Lydia said, grinning. "We have turned out, hundreds of us! Enough of us to stop the mills, I think!" She flashed Zellie a smile of triumph, then it faded. "But Mrs. Gird was waiting at the gates, scolding and shouting at us. Poor Plumy ran off weeping. And Abigale nearly turned back."

She brushed back strands of hair that had worked their way free of her bun and her eyes met Zellie's. "Keep watch at the window, will you?"

Then without waiting for an answer, Lydia dodged around Zellie and headed for her room. "Just tell me if you see Mrs. Gird coming, please," Lydia called over her shoulder. "She'll try to keep me here if she can."

Zellie didn't answer, but she glanced at the window and felt her hands go cold.

"Poor Plumy," Lydia was saying. "This was her first day, you know. She turned out, for my sake."

Zellie looked out the window and felt her hands start to sweat. She couldn't see anything but the river and the fields unless she moved closer.

"I left the petitions here in case most backed out," she said from her room, "so I wouldn't get them in trouble." She laughed. "But they didn't, so now I will get more to sign and then we will all march to the agent's house and give them to him!" There was a pause. "Do you see anyone coming?"

Zellie made herself take the first step. Breathing unevenly, she paused. She couldn't see anything close to the house yet. She needed to be right against the glass to see down into the yard.

"See anyone?" Lydia called again.

Zellie forced herself to stride forward, then looked downward. The yard was empty. She closed her eyes. "No! There's no one."

After a few seconds, she forced herself to look down again. Her stomach clenched, but she didn't step back. The yard was empty. She could hear the sound of Lydia opening her trunk. She shut her eyes. Her stomach was turning sick and she was sweating.

"Still clear?" Lydia called out once more. "The last thing I want is a fight with Mrs. Gird."

Zellie looked again and this time she kept her eyes open. "There's no one at all," she told Lydia.

But the instant she said it, she saw Mrs. Gird appear around the corner of the print works, walking fast, her arms swinging at her sides.

"Mrs. Gird is coming," Zellie said over her shoulder.

Lydia came rushing out of her room. "I hid my writing box so well, I had to take everything out of my trunk to get it out!"

The back door slammed closed and they both heard the sound of Mrs. Gird's keys jangling. Lydia went pale. "Oh, no. She's locking it! She'll never let me out in time to make my speech and—"

"Listen from up here," Zellie interrupted. "I'll get her into the storeroom. Then you slip past and go out the parlor window."

Lydia leaned forward and kissed Zellie on the forehead. "I will repay you somehow," she promised.

Zellie smiled, then grabbed her rags and the vinegar water and hurried down the stairs.

"Zellie!" Mrs. Gird shouted.

"I was just about to begin the second-floor washroom," she called out as she jumped down the last three stairs and saw Mrs. Gird coming up the hallway toward her.

"The girls are disgracing me and the mills and themselves!" Mrs. Gird hissed. Her face was flushed with anger. "And you knew it was today, didn't you?"

Zellie looked down at the floor. "None of all this is my business," she said meekly.

Mrs. Gird patted her head. "Just don't become what they are, Zellie." Zellie looked up and met her eyes. Mrs. Gird was frowning. "You have to know your place in this life, Zellie."

"Yesterday," Zellie said slowly, "I had trouble finding rags rough enough to really scour the basins clean."

Mrs. Gird narrowed her eyes.

"Hemp cloth would work," Zellie added. "Or a piece of frayed sisal rope."

Mrs. Gird's frown eased a little. "There's sisal rope in the storeroom."

Zellie looked up. "There is?"

Mrs. Gird sighed heavily. "I'll show you."

Zellie followed her down the hallway, and into the storeroom. Once they were inside, Zellie closed the door firmly behind herself.

"In here," Mrs. Gird said, reaching for the box Zellie had nearly spilled.

Zellie opened it and smiled, thinking about her grandmother again, but in a different way. Grandmamma would be proud of her, she was sure. She wouldn't like the fibbing, but she would like the idea of people standing up for themselves. And Grandmamma would be proud of how she had managed to stand by that window, too.

"Do you need a stronger soap?" Mrs. Gird asked.

"It might help," Zellie said quickly.

Mrs. Gird walked to the shelves along the way and pulled down a tin. "It'll eat your skin right off," she warned, "so if you use it, be careful and rinse quick."

Zellie nodded. "That's because it has more lye in it?"

Mrs. Gird nodded. "Lye and caustic soda. Don't get even a speck in your eyes."

Zellie nodded somberly. "My grandmother swore by vinegar water for most things."

Mrs. Gird turned and opened the door and Zellie held her breath. But there was no sound of footsteps. Lydia had made it.

"Thank you for the sisal rope, Mrs. Gird," Zellie

said, reaching to get the soap and a few clean rags.

Mrs. Gird made an impatient sound. "Just get about your work, Zellie. I know you lied to me about that meeting and I won't keep you on. Tomorrow morning I have a new girl coming in to help."

Zellie watched Mrs. Gird walk down the hall, heading toward the kitchen as a feeling of cold shock spread through her body. The heat of anger was quick to follow. She had done nothing wrong. She had done her work well.

Zellie looked down at the sisal rope and vinegar water. If she was to be let go, today was as good as tomorrow, wasn't it? If she left today, she could go hear Lydia's speech. She could try to find Plumy and calm her down. Then she would ask Miss O'Brien if she could pay a few pennies to sleep in the shop until she could find another position. The grocer might hire her to go through boxes of potatoes for a day or two.

Amazed at herself, but feeling the strange restlessness of the night before, Zellie put everything back in the storeroom. She would not be rude to Mrs. Gird, she decided. She would not lower her own pride that far. She ducked into the parlor and relatched the window Lydia had gone out. Then she headed for the kitchen.

"I think I will leave today, then," she announced politely.

Zellie Blake   129

Mrs. Gird turned slowly, a teacup steaming in her hand. "Pardon me?"

"I prefer to be let go today," Zellie said. "If you could just pay me for the days I worked, I will be on my way." Zellie was trembling, but she was determined, too.

"I can't see that I owe you anything," Mrs. Gird said in a low, tight voice.

The sound of someone knocking at the kitchen door made Zellie flinch. "Bertha!" A high, melodic voice sang out, then the knocking got louder. "Bertha Gird, are you home?"

Mrs. Gird walked to the door and unlocked it. "What do you want?"

Miss O'Brien smiled. "I brought you your hat since I was coming this way. I thought I might save you the walk into town."

Mrs. Gird glanced back at Zellie, her face still tight with anger. Zellie picked up her satchel from under the blankets. There was nothing else to get but her coat.

"I am not through with you," Mrs. Gird said harshly. Miss O'Brien tilted her head, but said nothing.

"If you would just pay me, please," Zellie repeated.

"Well, what a coincidence, Bertha," Miss O'Brien said. "I was hoping you'd settle for the hat today as well."

Mrs. Gird stared. "Come with me, I'll get my pocketbook."

"I'll wait here, if you don't mind," Miss O'Brien said.

Scowling, Mrs. Gird left the room, and Miss O'Brien smiled sweetly at Zellie. "You can leave your satchel at my shop and we could go join the girls if you like."

Zellie nodded, her heart lifting a little. "And if you know someone who might hire me . . ." Then she trailed off, hearing the sound of heavy footsteps approaching.

Mrs. Gird counted out Zellie's wages, forty cents for four days' work. Miss O'Brien accepted her money with a smile. Then they both went out the back door into the bright morning.

"Lydia said she thought you might be needing work," Miss O'Brien said. "I need an apprentice, Zellie." She started walking.

Miss O'Brien looked down at her. "You can take as many of the evening classes with the girls as you like, once your work is done."

Zellie looked into her face. "I can't pay for an apprenticeship."

Miss O'Brien veered toward town and Zellie followed her numbly, her heart thudding crazily.

"How about another barter," Miss O'Brien said. "You could do some of my housework—it's not much,

I am neat. But it's getting harder for me to keep things nice and run the shop, too. If you wouldn't mind working hard, then—"

"I wouldn't mind at all!" Zellie burst out.

"And we'll get you back in school, if you don't take to millinery work," Miss O'Brien said. "There's talk of opening a high school here, for all the children of Lowell." She held out her hand.

Zellie took it, glancing toward the sky, wondering if Grandmamma would mind if she loved this kind woman a little.

"I want to go hear Lydia speak," Miss O'Brien said.

"I had intended to, before you came," Zellie told her.

They both laughed, their breath making white fog in the cold air. Together they walked up the snowy street.

February 22, a Saturday, 1834

Plumy came into the shop this morning. She says she is thinking about going home, that the mills won't be running and that she can't bear the cost of staying if she cannot work. Miss O'Brien talked her into waiting at least a week. She thinks the turn-out won't last long. She also thinks it will fail, but that it will mean the next one will be better run and might succeed. "These things take time," she often says. I guess she is right.

Miss O'Brien has a spare room at her house and I have a bed! I intend to clean her little house and this shop until they shine. And I am going to practice the stitches she is showing me as well. She says neither of us has any other family. So perhaps we can make each other a little less lonely as well.

I am going to be all right, Grandmamma. I am. I miss you. But I am going to make my own way.